"WHAT IS IT

about stardropping that fascinates you so?" he demanded.

Making a helpless gesture, she closed her eyes and swayed a little. She said thinly, "Suppose you had a dream, a very important dream, in which you saw something you desperately wanted to remember—a bit of the future, say. And you woke up and you remembered you'd seen it, but not what it was.

"It's a little bit like that, except that what you can't quite remember is a matter of life and death. If you don't get back to it, you might as well cut your throat."

But as Agent Dan Cross knew, they didn't cut their throats. What happened to stardroppers was that they disappeared. There would be a sudden clap of noise—and the listener would have vanished—totally, permanently, inexplicably. It was now Dan's assignment to follow them—and return if he could.

THE STARDROPPERS

by
JOHN BRUNNER

DAW BOOKS, INC.
DONALD A. WOLLHEIM, PUBLISHER

1301 Avenue of the Americas
New York, N. Y. 10019

COPYRIGHT ©, 1972, BY BRUNNER FACT AND
FICTION, LTD.

ALL RIGHTS RESERVED.

A considerably shorter and different version of this novel appeared in 1963 under the title *Listen! The Stars!* and is copyright © 1963 by John Brunner.

COVER ART BY KELLY FREAS.

FIRST PRINTING SEPTEMBER 1972

3 4 5 6 7 8 9

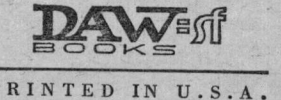

PRINTED IN U.S.A.

I

Glancing up from Dan Cross's passport to see whether the face in the picture matched the live version, the dark-uniformed immigration control officer said, "Stardropper?"

He could have meant Dan himself, or the instrument slung over his shoulder on a strap. Either way the answer ought to be yes. Dan nodded, and the immigration officer thawed noticeably.

"Been at it long?" he asked. "I'm a recent convert myself."

"So am I!" Dan said, feigning enthusiasm. To be precise, he had been issued the instrument four days ago. "What model do you have? This is a custom-built job, hand-assembled. A guy in LA turns them out."

"Wish I could spare the time to try it out," the immigration officer said with real envy. "Powerful, is it?"

"One of the best!"

Faintly through the heavy double walls of the airport building came the stunning roar of a Concorde supersonic taxiing toward takeoff. The man next in line behind Dan coughed and shuffled his feet impatiently. The immigration officer recollected himself and inquired how long Dan proposed to remain in Britain.

"I'm not sure," Dan said. "I'm on vacation. I guess I might be here about a month."

"I'll mark you down for two, then, just in case," the immigration officer said, and stamped the appropriate entry permit on the passport. Handing it back, he added, "I hope you enjoy your stay, sir."

Dan smiled mechanically, tucking the document back into an inside pocket, and moved on to collect his baggage from the "Nothing to Declare" sector of the customs hall. A porter answered his signal and loaded the bags on a humming electric trolley, offering to find Dan a taxi. Having told him yes, Dan walked on leisurely across the customs hall to a door labeled in dayglo letters TRANSIT LOUNGE—EXCHANGE FACILITIES—SHOPS—CONVENIENCES.

All very smart and impressive, this brand-new building: easily the equivalent of anything he'd seen in the States. The people, too, seemed brisk and alert. There was a sense of bustle in the air, and he heard a great deal of laughter. Dan was chary of first impressions, but he cautiously admitted that so far he thought he was going to like England.

He kept his long-jawed face set in the right expression for a curious tourist making his first visit here, but behind it his mind was very busy. It was one thing to be told that the stardropping craze had a stronger grip in Europe than at home; it was another to have had the point demonstrated within minutes of his arrival.

And here was another proof on top of the first. Standing just inside the brightly lit transit lounge was a wild-eyed young man, hair untidy, in jeans and a soiled cotton T-shirt, with a smear of grime on one cheek. As the newly arrived passengers filed through the door he was saying fiercely to one after another, "Klatch remoo! Listen to me, will you? *Klatch remoo!*"

The passengers scowled and brushed him aside in irritation. Against a nearby wall Dan saw a policeman and a member of the airport staff, watching the young man with serious faces but making no move to interfere. He wondered why not.

Then, the instant the young man caught sight of Dan's stardropper, he seized him by the sleeve and thrust his face close. His breath stank, as though he had lived on cigarettes for days past.

"You! Klatch remoo—what does that mean to you?"

"Nothing," Dan said shortly. "Take your hands off me."

"It *must!* Listen again. Klatch—"

Dan broke the grip on his arm with a twist toward the man's thumb. It looked as though the speed of the movement had made it painful. It was meant to. Angrily, Dan shot a glare at the policeman, who came forward at last.

"Mr. Grey!" he said sharply. "If you're going to be a

nuisance, we'll have to turn you out, understand? This is your last warning."

Grey let his hands fall hopelessly to his sides. A tear squeezed out of his eye and mingled with the grime on his cheek. He turned away and began to put his meaningless question to some one else.

Dan looked at the policeman. "What does he have to do to be classed as a nuisance?" he demanded.

"Well, he's expecting someone, you see, sir. Someone he says he heard of through his stardropper. You can hardly blame him, can you? After all, I see you're a fan yourself." The policeman gave a conspiratorial smile. "So am I, as a matter of fact."

"Yes, but surely he must be annoying a hell of a lot of people."

The policeman shrugged. "He's no great trouble, really. And the slightest chance, you know, is always worth taking."

"I guess so," Dan conceded; it seemed like the proper thing for a stardropper fan to agree, though he would have liked to ask what sort of chance the policeman had in mind. Much puzzled, he walked on across the lounge to an exchange counter.

While waiting to be served, he had plenty more reminders of the extent of the stardropper craze here. In glass-fronted display cases he counted four posters issued by firms making the things—two portable models, one fixed home installation, and a do-it-yourself kit. And on one of the padded benches nearby a girl sat waiting for her flight number to be called, meantime holding a stardropper on her knee with the earpiece half-hidden among her bright fair hair.

Building up a charge like the man Grey? Dan hoped not. She looked too pretty to go mad.

As his taxi spun down the Great West Road toward London he lit a cigarette and leaned back in his seat. Opening the case of his own instrument he stared at it for the twentieth time.

What the hell *were* these things all about, anyway?

About half the contents of the shallow square box made sense—the earpiece on its lightly coiled cord; the transistorized amplifier, conventional in design; and the power source. You could run a stardropper off anything within reason: flashlight cells were naturally commonest, or house current for the bigger models, but he'd seen at least one model advertised with a tiny built-in generator driven by clockwork. This one, though, as he'd told the immigration officer, was an expensive hand-crafted version; its power came from a fuel cell that converted butane gas directly into electricity, water vapor, and CO_2, just about the most efficient process yet devised.

So far, so good. What could be made of the rest? Item: one Alnico magnet on a brass slide; the slide was toothed and engaged with a worm. Item: one calibrated plastic knob on the same shaft as the worm, with millimeter gradations intended to be lined up against the point of a little chromed triangle on the side of the case. Item: one ultra-hard vacuum in a little aluminum box. There was a getter in the box to keep the vacuum swept, but the makers recommended trading it in for a new one about once a month. The butane tank—a standard cigarette-lighter refill—was guaranteed to last a year, minimum, and in practice might go for twice that long.

Add it up, and you got nonsense. But . . .

Dan lifted the earpiece and put it in. It was covered with foam rubber and tapered for a snug fit. He'd wondered already why full sets of earphones weren't supplied as standard with even an expensive stardropper like this one, but so far he hadn't found anyone able to answer the question. Apparently, within a couple of years, stardropping had developed its own brand of conservatism. Though it was of course true that there could be no stereo effect from a stardropper.

He switched on the power, twisted the calibrated knob at random, and waited. Nothing. He moved it a little farther, and a susurrus of noise began, like surf on a distant beach crossed with a pouring sound which rose steadily in pitch as the gurgle of water rises when a bottle is filled from a tap.

He closed his eyes attentively. One had to grant that the sound had an attractive quality. It hinted at meaning, like a voice speaking a foreign language. Or—more nearly

—like music, capable of conjuring up images and ideas but not communicating them as such.

This was not a good setting, though. After a little while the pleasant sound broke up in a gabble of shrill squawks, and he took out the earpiece quickly. Noticing the driver eying him in the rear-view mirror, he decided against another try and shut the case.

Obviously, he just wasn't with it. Plenty of his friends had joined the multiplying hordes of addicts, but whenever he had been persuaded to try out one of their instruments he'd found the experience merely interesting. Not fascinating. He'd taken the things for toys.

Yet, according to what he'd been told at his briefing in New York, they had in fact a subtle deadliness. Indeed, he'd been convinced of that this morning. At the end of the line might be a man like Grey, shouting desperate nonsense syllables at strangers and begging for a meaningful answer.

Asking what a stardropper really did seemed nearly as futile. Dan had been accorded the privilege of an interview with Berghaus himself, the only person with a theory to fit the facts, and he had hardly made heads or tails of the explanations he'd been offered. To judge by his helpless expression as he talked, even Berghaus couldn't be that much further forward.

Moreover, for a scientist he had been driven to use some appallingly unscientific-sounding terms: "psychic continuum," for example. There was apparently no alternative. This was simply an unscientific sort of phenomenon.

Point one: there was no conventional reason why a hard vacuum plus a magnet plus a power source should generate signals you could display on an oscilloscope, record on tape, feed through a speaker, or cause to jiggle needles back and forth across a dial.

Point two: the signals were *not* random noise. They were at least as highly organized—and therefore presumably information-full—as the most complex human speech. Information, as Berghaus had been at pains to emphasize even though Dan was well aware of the fact, was not *meaning;* it was a technical term related to degree of ordering. When the phenomenon had not yet been given its nickname, but was simply "the Rainshaw effect" after its discoverer, people naturally assumed the signals related in some way to periodicity of atomic or molecular vibration in the matter composing the equipment.

It was Berghaus who—after beating his head against the wall of the problem for months, along with uncountable others, both experts and ambitious laymen—found the extraordinary statistical correlation between the signals and the output of living nervous systems. The evidence was too technical for Dan, but he accepted Berghaus's word. So did millions of other people. The way Berghaus put it was this: "Just as the Zeeman effect, for example, informs an astronomer of the existence of a magnetic field surrounding a star, so these signals have characteristics suggesting an origin in an organized, percipient nervous system."

That was about a year after he proposed his now-famous theory of precognition. Evidence had finally piled up to such an extent that one was badly needed. To account for transfer of information future-to-past he invoked a space-equivalent for it to travel through, non-Einsteinian in that instantaneity there reacquired a definite meaning, and permitting knowledge of an event at moment x to become available at moment $x-y$ when it was not yet appreciable by the normal senses. Controversy was still going on, but so far the hypothesis was standing up well to criticism.

Reluctantly, Berghaus said, "It seems to me that these devices utilizing the Rainshaw effect may tap the space-equivalent which I have called the "psychic continuum" just as the mind of a man with ESP does."

His precognition theory had made Berghaus one of the most newsworthy of living scientists. Reporters accordingly descended on him in hordes to interrogate him about this new idea. Seeking an angle, one of them demanded why, if these signals originated in living minds, they could not be translated in some way, perhaps into words. Honesty compelled Berghaus to say that, if one followed the implications of his theory to the ultimate conclusion, one had to assume that all living, aware beings—human or otherwise—might have access to this timeless channel of information, and many of them might very well not employ words.

"Human or otherwise?" the reporter pressed him. "You mean creatures on other planets, under other stars?"

"If they exist, as they very probably do," Berghaus agreed. To him it was just an interesting possibility which could not be excluded on the basis of the evidence at hand.

But the reporter went away and coined the phrase "eavesdropping on the stars." Someone put out a cheap portable version of the Rainshaw device, intending it as an amusing gimmick. Someone else nicknamed it a stardropper.

And the world seemed suddenly to go insane.

II

Dan's organization was thorough. All the necessary preparations for his arrival had been attended to. He had been booked into a large modern hotel in Mayfair, where he checked in like any casual tourist, and he'd had time to eat lunch and move on to take coffee in a penthouse lounge overlooking the fine new towers of London before anything happened to remind him that other people could be thorough too.

At ten to three the lounge was nearly empty. It was therefore already a warning when the burly man walked through the door, came over, and took the other chair at the low table where Dan was sitting. Dan studied him. He saw a big-boned man, going bald, with a bristly brown mustache and red cheeks, who smiled when he found Dan's eyes on him.

"Special Agent Cross?" he said in a voice that did not carry nearly far enough to be overheard. And smiled again, more broadly.

So someone had goofed. But there wasn't much point in argument.

"Just plain mister," Dan said after a pause. "The organization has a title. We don't."

"I see. Well, you'll want to look at this." The burly man flipped an identification card from his pocket. It had his photo pasted to it, and underneath was typed "Hugo Samuel Redvers, Superintendent."

"Special Branch?" Dan said.

"Of course."

Dan sighed and handed back the card. "What can I do for you?" he said.

"Oh, just chat for a while. Answer one or two questions." Redvers settled more comfortably in his chair. A waiter passed with a tray and asked what he wanted; he ordered black coffee and a Havana.

"Such as?" Dan invited when the waiter had gone.

"Mainly, what brings you to Britain. Our man at the airport was slightly puzzled to see a Special Agency operative with one of those gadgets on his shoulder." Redvers waved at Dan's stardropper, lying on the table between them; the New York briefing for this trip had included a warning that all genuine stardropper fans took their beloved gadgets with them wherever they went, and he was determined to stay in character. "Your London office stoutly denied any knowledge of you, so I had no option but to come and talk to you personally. Cross isn't your real name, I take it?" he added in passing.

Dan shrugged. His real name was so far in the past he felt sometimes as though it had been just another of the dozen or so aliases he had used in ten years' work.

"Well, I won't press you," Redvers said after a pause. "I worry about what people do, not what name they choose to do it under. Well, Mr. Cross?"

The waiter delivered his coffee and cigar. He unscrewed its aluminum cylinder and sniffed appreciatively before lighting up.

Meanwhile Dan reached a decision. It was galling to have to declare any Agency interest to an outsider, but there seemed to be no help for it. Fortunately there was no special secrecy about his visit to London; it was classed as a Grade E mission, involving only such precautions as were necessary to preserve his future usefulness. So he said reluctantly, "Stardroppers."

"I thought it might be. Well, well." Redvers dumped his spent match in a handy ashtray. "I was wondering when you'd get into that particular act. Everyone else has been in it for months. Just fact-finding?"

"That's about the size of it."

"Then you're welcome to dig for any facts you can. And by the way: you needn't worry that being seen with me in public will foul you up. This is one of my working faces I have on. The name and rank are genuine, though, and so's the card—I had it made at the Yard this morning."

He looked for a reaction in Dan's face; Dan stonily denied him the pleasure of seeing any.

"We also checked your room for bugs, and I can assure you there aren't any. We knew which it was because we have a tap on the computer which centralizes hotel bookings in this village nowadays. All in all I feel rather pleased with myself today, which is why I'm treating myself to this cigar. Oh, I'm sorry—I should have asked if you'd like one. I imagine Havanas are something of a forgotten luxury as far as you people in the States are concerned."

"For a guy who knows all the answers, you're trying very hard to needle me," Dan said.

"I suppose I am. I'm sorry. I'll get back to the point. There are two major and several minor reasons why people get interested in the stardropping craze afflicting us. Among the minor reasons—well, commercial rivalry is one. The thing was invented here, and someone had the sense to tell Rainshaw he ought to file for a patent application, which incidentally makes fascinating reading. It's a prime example of doubletalk."

"I've read it," Dan grunted. But he agreed with Redvers's description. The application discussed a device for the generation of certain patterned electricial impulses independent of the known spectrum of radiant energy, and it was perfectly clear from the fudged wording of the text that neither the applicant—nominally, the company Rainshaw had been working for at the time of the discovery—nor anyone else had the vaguest notion what was being patented.

"You see what I mean, then," Redvers nodded. "Well, obviously stardropping is now big business, and the designs we've licensed—I mean we the British—are proving fantastically profitable. But the things are so easy to copy that we're having the devil's own trouble with pirate manufacturers, of course. Never mind that, though; I doubt your people would be interested in patent infringements. Then, as you probably know, we get a lot of problems with—well, I suppose one has to call them addicts, who are convinced someone has found a way to convert the signals into plain English and is hiding marvelous secrets from the world. Rubbish, of course, but it's turning into quite a serious social problem. That, though, is not really my business and I doubt if it's yours.

"Of the major reasons, there's what I consider this idiotic rivalry between the various nations to extract from stardroppers some knowledge which will make them masters of the world. Half the secret services on Earth seem to have sent people to London in the past year to grub around for hints and clues that might lead somewhere. But the Special Agency is the most fanatically internationalist of all the UN organizations, so unless you've turned your coat we can rule that out too. Which boils it down to one thing. You're here to confirm that somebody can't be found, and you'd far rather disprove the suspicion. Should I suggest a couple of likely names?"

He looked unblinkingly at Dan. A wisp of aromatic blue smoke drifted across his face.

"You do know all the answers," Dan said at length. "I apologize for that crack about needling me."

"I wish we did!" Redvers said with sudden heaviness. "One of the constables at the airport mentioned that you were taken aback by Grey's appearance, as though you hadn't been prepared for someone in his condition. I assure you that even if Grey was acting he's fairly typical of his kind."

"Acting? That wild-eyed guy yelling nonsense at people?"

"Oh yes, he's one of my men too. We've been living by our wits in this country for the past decade, Mr. Cross. We've become pretty good at it."

Professional admiration was getting the better of Dan's discomfiture. He said, "Maybe I shouldn't have bothered to fly over. I could have called you up and simply asked you."

"Hell, you'd have learned nothing. We're too close to the problem to make sense of it. What I'd like most is advice from one of these alien creatures people claim to hear in their stardroppers. Failing that, an outsider's view. And you're a stranger here, aren't you?"

"Yes, it's my first visit."

Redvers nodded. "But you must have been familiarized with the general situation—I know how thoroughly your operatives get briefed. Did your briefing by any chance include a suggestion that if someone like me started being nosy you weren't to object too strongly?"

"I was told you might be exceptionally cooperative with Agency representatives."

"We try to be, I promise you that. We appreciate your outfit's insistence on being on everyone's side instead of one side or the other—which of course is how we regard our own policy nowadays. It's a bit like walking a tightrope, though. This elderly continent of Europe is the battleground of the late twentieth century, and we're right in the bloody firing line. You know what I mean?"

"I guess I do. Not that anyone could tell just by looking."

"Oh, of course not. On the surface everything's fine. We're richer, better-housed, better-fed, better-educated than ever before in history, and we're climbing back up the ladder of the world's biggest trading nations at a rate of vertical knots. But what I'm talking about is in the mind. When we opted out of the arms race ten years ago the decision was called cowardice or treachery or worse, and I must admit I wasn't sure myself it was a good thing. And there was that uproar over adopting the Swiss citizen-militia defense system, which nearly brought down the government. But now I've been convinced by the results. No slums, no poverty, lowest crime rate in London of any city of its size in the world—you could imagine a policeman being pleased about that!"

"So what are these drawbacks you mentioned—in the mind, you said?"

Redvers wiped a fine gray cylinder of ash from his cigar. "Ah, yes. Maybe I can illustrate that with a little story. I once asked one of your compatriots how he liked it here, and he said it was a hell of a good place, bar two things—the nonstop political arguments in which we British try to figure out our own motives, and the knowledge that if things do ever come to the crunch both sides are going to hit this country on the principle of 'denying ground to the enemy.'" He gave a chuckle. "Well, you only die once. I hope. And, naturally, from a professional point of view the last ten years have been a troublesome time. At first we were staving off American intriguers who were sure we'd had a momentary brainstorm and would reconsider if they promised us enough dollar credit, and

Soviet intriguers who were sure neutrality was unthinkable and we were really intending to join the Soviet bloc. They were both wasting their time, but between them they contrived to turn this island into a sort of vast Tangier, a strategically sited zone where everyone and his uncle is plotting a *coup d'état*. Life isn't dull, but the risk of ulcers is on the high side.

"And that, according to the psychologists, is why stardropper was taken up so avidly. People, they maintain, are desperate for reassurance because they're being denied security, and they'll grab at even so slim a chance as the hope of knowledge from the stars. If that were the whole story, of course, it would be fine."

"I've heard that theory before. Is it sound?"

"Possibly. On the other hand the country where stardropping is most widespread, after this one, isn't in Europe at all. It's India. The Japanese get out this very cheap solar-powered model, and people go out with loads of them on incredible ramshackle vehicles—I've seen pictures —and in the villages they club together to buy the largest and loudest they can afford. Then they put the earpiece in a washtub or something to act as a resonator, and bob's your uncle: every man his own guru. It's alleged to appeal to the religious instinct of the people. Take your choice of explanations. There are enough to go around, heaven knows!"

He realized suddenly he had forgotten his coffee, and gulped the whole cupful down at once.

"How are things doing in the States?" he continued after a pause.

"I have the impression the craze is six months to a year behind the peak it's reached in Britain," Dan answered. "It has a strong hold on the West Coast, but all kinds of fads have always flourished there. In the East it's mainly young people and Greenwich Village types who are hooked, while the Midwest is barely touched—apart from universities, I mean. Even there, I think you have a worse student problem than we do, isn't that right?"

"That's a very bad area indeed," Redvers confirmed. "One hears every day about the number of kids who are dropping out—stardropping out," he amended with a grimace. "It's mainly the sensitive, highly intelligent kids who are affected, too. They're suffering the low-grade version of the ultimate addiction, which can cause you to lose interest in your home, your job, your family, your other hobbies. . . . But of course the insanity isn't the worst part of it."

"Not the worst part of it?" Dan echoed. "What in hell *could* be worse, if you were right in saying Grey was based on a typical—ah—addict?"

"Oh, the fact that people do disappear."

Redvers uttered the words so casually that Dan wondered whether he had heard right. He could not stop himself from jerking with surprise.

"Yes, Mr. Cross," Redvers said soberly. "They disappear. And judging by your reaction I take it I was right about the main purpose of your visit?"

"Well, yes, I'm here to check out some rumors. But—"

"But what makes me believe such a fantastic story?"

Dan nodded.

"We've documented twenty cases where we can't shake the witnesses. They say—they swear—that people known to them have literally and physically vanished, usually with a noise like a door slamming. Up till now we've prevented any reputable news agency from picking up such stories, but we can't stop the rumors."

Dan's palms were slippery with sweat. He said, "What do these—these witnesses think about what they claim to have seen?"

"What you'd expect: that these were people who'd discovered mystic alien abilities through the stardropper and went to put them to use."

"And you honestly believe them?"

"No. Not yet. But I have a sneaking suspicion I shall have to eventually. And if this is true, of course, it's a pretty explosive fact. A power of instantaneous displacement, if it could be brought under control, could be put to use as a weapon: imagine eliminating the need to deliver H-bombs by plane or missile! Surely that if anything might tempt one of the nuclear nations into a pre-emptive strike once they were convinced the 'other side' was on the verge of such a breakthrough. I presume this is why your people are investigating the rumors?"

Dan nodded. The Agency had one sole purpose: to identify threats to the peace of the world and ruthlessly cancel them out. For example, within the past year two prime ministers had died, one of a heart attack and the other of a cerebral embolism. Social psychologists had plotted graphs and said, "Such a man is not sane, and a lunatic in his position could start a war."

"Well, for my part I'm very glad to see you," Redvers went on. "And any help I can give, I certainly will. To begin with, perhaps you'd like to meet Rainshaw?"

"I wouldn't object."

"Fine, I'll arrange that as soon as possible. And I'll keep in touch during your stay, make sure you don't run into any difficulties. Maybe you'll come up with a practical way of cooling the situation. Lord knows we need some bright ideas!"

He stubbed his cigar, rose, and offered his hand. "Well, it's been a pleasure making your acquaintance, Mr. Cross. Do contact me at the Yard, won't you, if there's anything else I can do?"

Feeling slightly numb, Dan shook hands with him and watched him stride toward the exit.

I was never so politely told I was incompetent.

Gradually he began to relax. The superintendent struck him as the kind of man one could respect for being clever without suspecting him of being cunning. That trap at the airport, for instance, had been as brilliant a stratagem as Dan had ever seen. He hadn't given a thought to how closely Grey could study his face, hear his voice, and even feel his clothes while howling his nonsense.

And he did know all the answers. It was precisely those rumors that stardropper enthusiasts were vanishing which had brought Dan across the Atlantic. Now Redvers had told him of twenty well-documented cases, hard though that was to accept. Which implied that even if they had opted out of the arms race, these people—by turning stardroppers loose on the world—had lit the fuse on a sizable bomb of a brand-new kind.

III

Shaking his head, Dan turned to the table beside him and picked up the gaudy-covered magazine on which his stardropper was lying. He had spent the flight from New York reading a stack of these magazines; the stardropper craze had probably set some sort of record for the speed with which it had produced clubs of enthusiasts, hobby magazines, and do-it-yourself kits.

This was the glossiest he had found. It was called *Starnews* and it was published in California. On the cover, a line of puff claimed it was "The FIRST and still the BEST magazine for stardroppers." But, considering it ran to 112 large slick pages, it was remarkably uninformative. At the beginning, twenty pages of advertisements were interspersed with chatty social news and correspondence between people asking advice, recounting their experience with various makes of instruments, and singing the praises of their own favorite settings on the dials.

Then the meat of the issue: articles, reviews of equipment, and progress reports by serious researchers including one or two working for big name companies, all illustrated in color. The tone of the articles was either technical or semi-mystical. One contribution aimed at proving that the truths of astrology had foreshadowed the stardropper, with a passing reference to Nostradamus, but the editor had put in a box on the second page a notice that contributors' opinions didn't reflect those of the magazine.

The most notable impressions Dan had gleaned from this and similar publications were, first, the overtone of respect in most of the articles, such as is heard in the voice of a man discussing a religion he admires without belonging to, and second, the total absence of what he regarded as the two most crucial points about the entire subject.

No one so much as questioned the corrections of Berghaus's theories. It was taken for granted that stardropper signals were really a way of overhearing alien minds at work.

And there was no mention of anyone having disappeared.

Granted, as he had told Redvers, the grip the craze now had in the States was nothing compared to the situation here—but there were plenty of items of British news, and advertisements from British companies. Surely, if there were any solid foundation for these wild stories of people vanishing, you'd expect to find at least one reference to it.

Sighing, he leafed through the advertisement section at the end until he found what he was after: a full-page insertion by an Oxford Street, London, store. If it advertised on this scale in a magazine from Los Angeles it might be a good place to start asking questions.

Behind curved nonreflecting glass a six-foot star turned slowly, hung apparently on nothing. Beneath it a dozen recent-model stardroppers were displayed on red velvet; the display was as restrained as that of an expensive jewelry store. In place of a door there was an air-curtain. Dan stepped through.

Her feet hushing on deep-piled carpet, a pretty milky-chocolate girl came up to him. She wore a fashionable high-collared yellow shirt and full black culotte pants to mid-calf, but to identify her to the customers a miniature duplicate of the star in the window was pinned on her bosom.

"Good afternoon, sir!" she said cheerfully. "Can we help you?"

Dan lifted his stardropper. "I think my vacuum's gone soft," he lied straight-faced. "Do you keep trade-in tanks for this model?"

The girl took the instrument from him and looked it over. "Oh yes. If you'd like to come to the back counter I'll get you one."

"Thank you."

He followed her slowly, looking around. There was no doubt this must be a profitable business. The layout was too subdued to be called lush, but everything had a rich look. Even the stock-display shelves down either side were covered in the same red velvet he had seen in the window. Four other customers were present. A middle-aged man and woman sat side by side in the corner farthest from the door, listening jointly to a type of stardropper Dan hadn't run across before: it was fitted with two pairs of double earpieces, like twin stethoscopes, connected to the same unit. His mouth quirked at this example of togetherness.

Neither of them moved the entire time he was in the store.

And at the counter two young Chinese were leafing through a catalog and asking technical questions of a youthful clerk. During his brief walk from the hotel he had noticed how many Chinese tourists there were around, but according to his briefing stardropping was considered an antisocial time-wasting habit in all the Maoist countries, so it was surprising to find them here.

The girl came back with the fresh tank of vacuum. "Shall I fit it for you?" she inquired.

"Well—thanks very much."

She attended to the job deftly. "We haven't seen you before, have we?" she said conversationally. "Are you an American?"

"That's right. I saw your spread in *Starnews* and found out your place was handy to my hotel. Say—uh—something else you might be able to do for me. I'm new to this, but I'm very interested, and I'd kind of like to get in touch with a club while I'm in London. Meet some people doing serious work in the field."

"We can certainly help you there," the girl said, and shut the case with a click. "That's one pound fifty pence, please. We run a club for our regular customers, with weekly meetings. Our manager, Mr. Watson, is the chairman. Would you like me to ask if he could have a word with you?"

"That'd be very kind of you," Dan said, laying down three of the curious seven-sided coins he kept wanting to call half-pounds.

"I'll just make sure he's in his office. Perhaps you'd like to glance through our catalog while you're waiting?"

She placed a fat looseleaf binder before him containing at least a hundred pages of thick shiny paper, and he hefted it in surprise. He said, "How many different models do you stock, for heaven's sake?"

The girl gave a faint smile. "Around sixty. But there are nearly two hundred in production. Have a seat, why don't you? That's too heavy to read standing up."

She waved him to a cluster of imitation Louis Quinze chairs in what looked like real gilt, and he headed for them, glancing at the various instruments on the shelves that he passed and wondering whether they were as different internally as they were externally. Just about every known kind of finish had been applied to the cases, from plain plastic through engine-turned stainless steel to the ultra-luxurious models in fine-quality leather, like his own He particularly liked one molded in imitation ivory, a copy of a medieval Indian spice box.

Sitting down, he opened the catalog and found a blurb on the first page, which he read thoughtfully. It ran:

> *We live in a strange era. Until recently, death was our closest neighbor; we walked with him, day in, day out. He has not gone from us, but since the discovery of the stardropper we have learned that life is as close as death and no more distant than the turn of a dial.*
>
> *Some people seek in the sounds of a stardropper new knowledge of the universe. These are the serious students whose work becomes their life. Others ask no more than the comfort of experiencing for themselves the signals which, scientists tell us, indicate that other beings in the cosmos live, and think, and maybe love.*
>
> *Whichever category you fall into, we are at your service.*
>
> ### COSMICA LIMITED

Well, that was one way of looking at it. . . .

Behind him a voice said, "Well, well! One of Harry Binton's hand-built jobs! And very nice too."

Dan glanced around. The speaker was a man of forty-odd, smart in maroon and black, and he was holding out his hand. Rising, Dan said, "You must be Mr. Watson."

"That's right. Sit down, sit down. That is one of Harry's instruments, isn't it, Mr.—?"

"Cross. Dan Cross. Yes, this is a Binton. You know him?"

"We're his agents in this country. Very fine work he does. Though—oh, I'm probably parochial, but in general I prefer British designs. No doubt about the efficiency of his products, of course; there's no more powerful model you can hang on a strap. Have you tried many other instruments?"

"As a matter of fact, no," Dan admitted. "I got hooked by a friend just recently, and I picked out a Binton because I saw a good notice for this instrument in *Starnews*."

Watson cocked his head on one side. "A little too powerful for a novice, possibly. People can get disheartened if they start with too advanced an instrument. Let me show you a Gale and Welchman—there's a setting on those that can be a revelation. It's only a dry-cell model, and one of the cheapest we recommend, but astonishing value for the price."

He reached to a high shelf and took down a large plain instrument in a white case. Setting it on his knee, he passed Dan the earpiece.

"Tell me when I get the setting right," he said. "It's usually between fifteen and sixteen on this scale, but of course it varies from one to another. Getting anything?"

This earpiece was bigger and less comfortable than his own; Dan held it in place with one finger and obediently closed his eyes, the very picture of an eager new stardropping fan.

"I think that's it," Watson murmured.

Dan listened hard. Somewhere at the back of his mind a drum was beating. A slow rhythm built up from it, quickened, grew louder. A melodic instrument joined in—or was it a voice singing? No, it was more like a joyful shout. The drumbeat was changing to a tramp of feet (changing, or had he mistaken it at the start?), yet it wasn't marching feet at all. It was the pumping of a huge heart, and signified life, awareness, vigor. Even violence! For it was the rumble of an earthquake at work on the building of mountains, and the shouting was the scream of rocks being ground upward past their ancient bedfellows out of the once-level plain—

It stopped, and he opened his eyes. He was shaking all over. Watson was smiling like a Cheshire cat; his hand rested on the adjusting knob, which he had turned from its setting.

"Well?" he said.

"You're right, it's amazing." Dan wiped his perspiring forehead with a tissue, reflecting that if any of his friends had shown him that one, he might be a real enthusiast by now.

"*That's* what stardropping is all about, you realize." Watson patted the instrument he held, like a pet animal. "This model had an excellent repertoire. I've known people who've gone on to build big fixed installations and haven't brought themselves to trade in their original Gale and Welchmans because they like the repertoire so much."

A reference encountered in *Starnews* crossed Dan's memory. He said, "You can't get that on any other instrument, then?"

"Oh no. Why, even Gale and Welchman turn out the occasional failure without the setting I just demonstrated. But I wouldn't sell one here, of course. It would be unfair to the customers."

He pointed to Dan's copy of *Starnews*, visible in the side pocket of his jacket. "You'll find a lot of correspondence in there between people who are trying to pair up signals received on different instruments. At present the system of calibration is arbitrary—not to say chaotic —and even one repeatable signal would serve as a valuable standard. Our club does a certain amount of research into this kind of thing, incidentally, and I gather you were asking about it."

"That's right. Obviously there's a lot for me to learn, and I don't want to waste my time in London."

"Here, then." Watson produced a small card from his pocket and wrote his name on the back before handing it to Dan. "We meet every Wednesday, as you see. Please join us tomorrow if you like. There's a small entrance fee to cover the cost of renting the room, and if you want to come regularly you pay a subscription of ten pounds. But you'll be welcome as a guest tomorrow night."

The card said CLUB COSMICA and gave the address of a pub called the Hunting Horn in the same postal zone as this store. From the other side Dan saw that Watson's given name was Walter. He put it in his wallet.

"Thanks very much. What time should I arrive?"

"About eight. We have a demonstration this week, so it'll pay to be prompt if you want to be sure of a good seat."

Outside the store, Dan almost fell over a girl sitting on the ground. She had the earpiece of a stardropper in, and with eyes closed and mouth open she was chalking a series of spiral lines on the pavement. Half a dozen passersby paused to inspect what she was doing, but by now the spirals covered one another so heavily it was impossible to make out the order in which they had been drawn. Presumably she was hoping someone would recognize the pattern and speak to her. No one did.

In a drugstore window, as he approached Marble Arch, he saw single earplugs on sale, labeled TO AID CONCENTRATION WHILE STARDROPPING.

Waiting to cross at a stoplight, he heard a boy in his late teens hailing a friend: "Dropped any good stars lately?"

Then a man of about sixty, smartly dressed in dark blue, went by pushing a handcart, which Dan guessed might be an old hawker's barrow. On its cracked, dirty boards was a huge stardropper in a shiny cabinet, a heavy home-model type. From its speaker oozed a sound like something flat and clumsy being moved about in thick mud, sucking and plopping. The man had his head cocked on one side, frowning fiercely. Behind him followed five or six youths and girls, also neatly dressed, though they were keeping to the sidewalk. Every time a driver hooted a complaint at being balked by the slow pushcart, they waved their fists at him threateningly.

One of the girls had a look on her face like a saint in ecstasy, and the boy with her was having to lead her by the hand. Next to her was another girl, who was clearly getting nothing from the sound and kept shooting envious looks at her luckier companion. She had short-cut black hair and a peaked gamine face with a sullen mouth, and she wore the leisure clothes currently popular with both sexes—a high-collared shirt and checked pants.

What it was that made Dan single her out from the group as it approached, he didn't know. But what attracted her attention to him was obvious. It was his stardropper.

She fell out from among her companions, as though giving up in despair, and came toward where Dan was standing, fumbling in her pocket. She withdrew her hand very swiftly as she pushed by.

A knife blade flashed. It severed the strap of Dan's stardropper. She caught hold of it, tugged it loose, and took to her heels.

IV

Half a dozen people saw the act and attempted to stop the girl, but the crowd around her was dense and she had eeled out of reach in a moment. If she had picked on anyone but a trained Agency operative she might have got away with it; as it was, he didn't catch up with her until he'd followed her clear across the multiple traffic streams of Park Lane and well into Hyde Park.

Once out here on the open grass, he could keep her in sight all the time, and it simply became a matter of wearing her down. It didn't take long. As soon as she saw he was still on her track, she gave up. He had expected her to distract him by throwing the stardropper down and making off without it; instead, she just stopped, panting like a bellows and plainly exhausted even by such a short run.

He came up to her, wondering at the defiance in her dark eyes, and noted how undernourished she looked—a strange sight in this prosperous city. He said nothing.

After a moment she hefted the stardropper in both hands, its cut strap trailing on the ground. As though she had read his mind, she said, "No, I wouldn't have thrown it away. It might have been broken."

Her voice was flat and emotionless. Dan went on looking at her steadily.

A few seconds of that and her self-control broke. She thrust the stardropper toward him violently. "Here you are, then!" she said with shrill impatience.

He made no move to take the instrument. Confused, she bit down on her lower lip. A crafty look crossed her face.

"You—uh—you aren't going to turn me in," she suggested.

"No, I don't think so," Dan said. At the words she brightened visibly.

"Would you . . . ?" She had to swallow and start again. "Would you let me try it out?" she ventured, folding her arms over the stardropper and pressing it tight to her chest. "That's all I wanted it for, I swear it was. To use it! I didn't mean to *sell* it or anything!"

Dan sighed. This was just about the most peculiar thief he had ever run across.

Licking her lips, she added, "If you want anything—I mean, I'll do anything you want if you let me just try your 'dropper. I need it so badly, honest I do!" Her voice broke on the last phrase.

Dan moved his right arm like a striking snake and caught hold of the broken strap, twitching the instrument out of her grasp before she could react. He brought it up short an inch above the ground, watching her face.

The expression of horror which overcame her was genuine; it was like a junkhead's, seeing someone threaten to tip away his entire stash of heroin. So here was one of the young addicts mentioned in his briefing, whom Redvers had also referred to.

"You louse," she said when she recovered. "Did you pull wings off flies when you were a kid?"

There was too much pathos in her attempted dignity for Dan to answer at once. He began to knot the strap of the instrument together.

"If you need stardropping that bad," he said at length, "why don't you have one of your own?"

"I did have. My mother broke it a week ago. Said I spent too much time with it. So I walked out. But I don't have any money for a new one, and it's sheer *hell* being without, because I was getting somewhere. I know I was getting somewhere. I'd tried for months and I'd finally begun to make it."

"So you ran away from home. Where are you living now?"

"It's none of your business!" she snapped. "Nor anybody else's. I'm sixteen—it's not illegal!" Then, relenting, she added, "With—with some friends. They run a commune. In Hackney."

"Don't any of these friends of yours have stardroppers they could lend you?"

"Of course!" Scornfully. "All of them do. That's what the commune's for, so we can 'drop as much as we like without anyone bugging us. But I've tried them all, and they don't suit me. So I came into town today to see if I could find a place selling secondhand ones, work out how much I'd have to spend to get a model like what I had before. Only there aren't many secondhand 'droppers, and the ones I did see were all types I know don't do anything for me. Then this old man came by with the cart, and I thought I'd listen to his for a bit, see if that was any good, and it wasn't, and then I saw yours and I realized that wasn't any of the makes I've tried. I'm sorry, but—oh, I'm going through absolute bloody torture. Look!"

She held one thin hand out in front of her. It shook like a wind-tossed leaf.

"What model did you have?"

"Just a cheap one—a Gale and Welchman—but it was very good."

So her pitiable state was due to Watson's pet brand of stardropper, was it? Dan scowled. How had things been allowed to progress to this point? On this showing, stardropping ought to be legislated against, like a dangerous drug.

"What is it about stardropping that fascinates you so?" he demanded, not really expecting a coherent answer.

"How can I tell you if you don't know? You're a 'dropper yourself, aren't you?"

"To me it's no more than mildly interesting. I could live without it. Why can't you?"

Making a helpless gesture, she closed her eyes and swayed a little. She said thinly, "Suppose you had a dream, a very important dream, in which you saw something you desperately wanted to remember—a bit of the future, say. And you woke up and you remembered you'd seen it, but not what it was. It's a little bit like that, except that what you can't quite remember is a matter of life or death. If you don't get back to it, you might as well cut your throat."

"Or starve, hm?" Dan suggested. "When did you last eat anything?"

"Oh... yesterday, I guess. Maybe the day before. I'm too worried to be hungry."

Dan looked past her. Among trees a short distance away a flag fluttered limply in the breeze, bearing a trademark of a catering company, and people could be seen coming away from that direction carrying sandwiches and cartons of soft drinks.

"I'll make a deal with you," he said. "There's a snack-bar over there, isn't there? You come with me and eat something, and afterward you can borrow my instrument for a while. Fair?"

She paused before replying, her dark eyes enigmatic. Eventually she said, "I told you, I'm sorry I tried to steal your 'dropper. But you don't have to make me feel so small, damn you. Cosmica isn't far from here. I'll go there and pretend I have some money to buy a 'dropper and see if they'll let me try some out for a while."

He sighed and took her by the arm. She didn't resist.

Even with coffee in one hand and sandwiches in the other and on her lap, she couldn't tear her eyes away from his stardropper for more than seconds together. He was sure that if he'd allowed her she would have thrown the food aside and put the earpiece in immediately.

"What's your name?" he said when she had wolfed two chicken sandwiches and emptied her paper cup.

"Lilith Miles."

"And you said you're sixteen. So I guess you're in school."

"Was. I quit."

That fitted, too, thought Dan. She went on, "I had this bargain with my mother, you see—I said I'd keep up with my schoolwork if she let me go on 'dropping. Not that what they tell you at school seems very important after you begin to get results from a 'dropper. Then she went back on what she promised, and smashed it up while I was out. I suppose I should have taken it with me. I usually used to. So, like I told you, I walked out."

"You keep talking about these results you were starting to get. What sort of results?"

Lilith made a frustrated gesture. "Things that don't go into words. And yet they make this weird kind of sense!

Oh, sometimes you do get very clear impressions, like a friend of mine got news that his father was going to die in an accident, but that doesn't happen very often, and anyhow it's not terribly important."

"I'd have thought death was pretty important," Dan said, lighting a cigarette. The day was bright, and people in bright clothes, many with children, were coming and going on the bright-green grass of the park, but the air felt cold on his skin.

"Sure it is. But it seems to be completely random, so what's the good of it? If you could rely on it happening regularly, that'd be different."

A valid point, Dan conceded. He said after a pause, "Some people go out of their minds, don't they?"

"Oh, plenty." She didn't seem to find the thought disturbing, which was if possible more shocking than what had gone before. "I guess they get stuck halfway. They get impatient, and can't wait to see the whole thing clear. Another friend of mine—she started fixing nonsense names on things and went around telling them to everybody, thinking they'd mean something. But of course they didn't. What comes out of a 'dropper simply doesn't belong in words!"

"But aren't you frightened that the same thing might happen to you?"

"No. It's like being killed in a car crash—you always think of it happening to someone else."

Which wasn't in itself a reason for taking crazy risks, Dan countered silently. He said, "I keep hearing stories about people who—who actually disappear. You too?"

A note of real envy crept into her voice. "They're the ones, aren't they?" she said. "They've got it and gone!"

"Where?"

"If I knew, wouldn't I be there too?" She looked at him, puzzled. "Say, I think you're putting me on!"

"I'm not. I honestly want to know your views. These people who've disappeared—did you know any of them?"

She shook her head.

"Then how did you hear about them?"

"Oh, everybody knows. You don't talk about it much. It's—sort of scary, follow? But that's *it*, that's the thing."

"Well..." Dan was groping for the right questions now.

"Well, what do people think may happen when someone disappears?"

"Oh, there are lots of theories," she said scornfully. "But me, I suspect it's something you can't understand until you get there yourself. Sometimes, listening to a 'dropper, you *almost* see how it could be done. You nearly get it. You make to catch hold, and it's gone again. It's like trying to catch a wriggly fish with your bare hands. You miss it ten times, a hundred times, but you get closer, you get better at it. You have to keep plugging away. You have to be so hungry for fish, you daren't get impatient; you have to keep calm, and concentrate, and stick at it. Can I try your 'dropper now?"

She tossed her coffee cup in a litter basket and reached for the instrument without awaiting an answer. Reluctantly, Dan surrendered it to her.

"This is a beaut!" she said in an impressed tone. "I thought it looked pretty good from the outside, but inside it's a dream, isn't it? I never used a fuel-cell model before. How do you switch on the power?"

He showed her the little sliding switch on the cell, and she tucked the earpiece into position, leaned back on the bench, and closed her eyes.

All the premature hardness went out of her face; the taut, nervous lines beside her sullen mouth faded and she began to smile a little. Dan watched her anxiously. He had an obscure sense of guilt, as though he were conniving at the corruption of a minor, and yet it was pleasant to see the change that had come over her.

She moved the adjuster knob with such patient care, seeking the right setting with such miniscule motions, that at first he did not realize she had stopped turning it. Then he began to wonder how long he should let her continue, whether it was dangerous to interrupt her, and even— the thought was ridiculous, but it crept eerily into his mind—whether she might here and now find what she was after . . . and vanish.

He shivered. It was growing genuinely cool as evening approached, and the rush-hour traffic was filling all the nearby streets. But that wasn't what caused it. He lit another cigarette and compelled himself to be as patient as Lilith. Sometimes the people coming and going around the park gave a second glance as they passed the bench, but not often. Lilith was far from the only person in sight listening to a stardropper; idly, he counted seven in direct view.

Almost half an hour elapsed, and he was preparing himself to take the risk of turning the knob and taking the instrument away, when she stirred and opened her eyes. She looked vaguely disappointed. Removing the earpiece, she closed the box with a sigh.

"It didn't work out," Dan said.

"Oh, it did!" she exclaimed. "It was great! This is a far more powerful instrument than my old one, but it's the first I've tried which does anything at all for me apart from that."

"What difference does the extra power make?" Dan asked, thinking of the confused state of the "art" reflected in those letters he'd read in *Starnews*.

"It feels—uh—harder to sort out what matters," Lilith said, and bit her lip. After a moment, she shrugged. "But it was great anyway. Right now I simply can't concentrate any more. But I'd love to try it again sometime. Please say I can!"

Dan hesitated. If this kid started to pester him for the use of his stardropper, she could clearly become a damned nuisance. On the other hand, his brief required him to investigate the impact of the craze in as much detail as possible, so it would be very useful to have an entrée to this commune she'd said she was staying at, where everyone was involved with stardropping. He spread his hands and nodded.

Grinning like a monkey, she jumped to her feet. "I'm terribly sorry about—about what happened," she said. "If I'd had any sense I'd just have walked up and asked you, wouldn't I? Can I try again in the morning?"

"On one condition."

"That I don't become a nuisance? I promise."

This kid was definitely a character, whatever kind of mess she'd got herself into. "That's right," Dan said. "So how can I reach you?"

"It'd be easier for me to reach you, I think—we don't have a phone in the house where I'm living. Tends to ring at the worst possible moment, if you follow me. You are an American, aren't you?"

"Yes."

"So I suppose you're in a hotel. Which?"

He told her, and she walked off across the grass with her hands in her pockets, humming a cheerful tune. After a little she began to skip on every other step, as though joy had made her too light to stick to the ground.

When she was out of sight, he opened the stardropper again and, out of curiosity, put in the earpiece. The knob was still on the setting which had given her so much pleasure. He upped the power and waited.

No good. What he heard sounded like a dozen banshees having an orgy, a pattern of shrill acid whistling noises. It was a setting he'd chanced across the first time he tried out the instrument, and had disliked intensely.

Now Lilith had owned a Gale and Welchman, and he'd been convinced already that that instrument had a particularly attractive setting in its repertoire. How could this unbearable racket relate to what Watson had demonstrated at Cosmica? More: how could it conceivably become meaningful?

Well, he had learned a lot as a result of his chance meetings today, there was no denying. It was probably appropriate to the whole curious muddle that the more he learned the more confused he became.

The hell with it for today, anyhow. If he acquired any more contradictory data before he'd relaxed with a good dinner and a night's sound sleep, he'd develop a dreadful case of mental indigestion.

V

He was shaving next morning when the phone sounded. A familiar voice followed his touch on the attention switch.

"Morning, Cross. I've arranged for you to see Dr. Rainshaw today, as I promised."

"Morning, Redvers. That's very kind of you. Ah—I don't want to seem unappreciative, but are you sure this is *purely* in the interests of cooperation?"

Redvers gave an engaging chuckle. "I told you yesterday, Cross: we desperately need an outside opinion on the muddle we've drifted into, and you're the best outsider we have on hand. Tell me, incidentally: has Watson invited you to Club Cosmica this evening?"

"Don't tell me you have that store of his bugged!"

"No. But I gather you called there yesterday, and Watson is utterly predictable. He talks every customer he can into signing on. By the way, in case you were wondering, it appears to be a genuine organization, not a commercial racket. Some of the most respectable people working in the stardropper field are regular attenders at its meetings."

"You must be very interested in Watson," Dan said. "Why?"

"For the same reason that I assume took you to his store. The biggest firm of its kind in the country is an obvious place to keep in touch with what's going on. Look, I imagine you haven't had breakfast yet, so I won't keep you from it. Dr. Rainshaw is at a government research station in Richmond, on the fringe of London. If I call for you at ten sharp, we'll be in plenty of time to keep the appointment I've made."

Promptly at ten Redvers arrived, driving not an official car but—presumably—his own, a small electrice-blue Healey steam convertible of a type Dan had expected to see all around London, knowing the demand for them, but which were still rare in Britain because so many were being exported to pollution-conscious California. Having left a message with a supercilious and puzzled reception clerk, to say that if a Miss Lilith Miles called she should be given an apology for his absence, he went out to the sidewalk. On the point of getting into the car, he heard his name called shrilly.

And there was Lilith, hurrying toward him with a suspicious expression.

"Just a moment," Dan told Redvers under his breath, and turned to greet the girl with a smile.

"Sorry!" he exclaimed. "I have to go see someone unexpectedly. I left a message at the desk asking you to call back later."

"Ohhh—I." For an instant he thought she was going to hit him; her fists doubled shut and her mouth turned sharply down at the corners. But she recovered, and said in a moderate tone, "You did make me a promise, though —didn't you?"

"Sure I did. And I'll keep it too. But this is important, and I didn't hear about the appointment until this morning."

"What's the trouble?" Redvers called from the car. Dan explained in a few words. Listening, Lilith looked so woebegone it was almost funny. When he had finished, she broke in before Redvers could answer.

"If you're going somewhere on business, you won't need your instrument, will you? Can't you just lend it to me?"

"I shouldn't," Redvers said, addressing Dan. "Not if you want to see it again."

She favored him with a furious glare.

"Well . . ." Dan gave a shrug. "I'm on my way to see Dr. Rainshaw, the man who discovered the whole thing. You wouldn't want me to miss a chance like that, would you?"

"Goodness, no!" Lilith's expression changed magically. "Oh, you lucky devil! I'd give anything to—Hey! Can I come along?"

"No, you cannot," Redvers said crossly. "Come on, get

in! I'm likely to be booked for blocking traffic if I stay here much longer, and that'll be embarrassing."

"One moment," Dan requested, his mind racing. "Ah . . . I have it. Redvers, we're not likely to be at this place all day, are we?"

"I hope not. I'm figuring on being back at the office before lunch."

"In that case . . ." Dan dug out the memo book he always carried and felt for a pen. "Lilith, give me the address you're staying at, and I'll call around this afternoon. And that's a firm promise, okay?"

"And you'll tell me about meeting Dr. Rainshaw?"

"Well, naturally."

"Okay, then." Though it was clear from her face she regarded this as a second-best. She reeled off the address and added that there was a bus which passed the door, and he smiled at her and got into the car at last. The instant he was settled, Redvers let off the brake and shot into the traffic.

Glancing at his rear-view mirror, which showed the despondent Lilith standing miserably on the pavement, he said, "Going in for cradle-robbing now, are you?"

"Hardly. But I feel sorry for her. She's in a hell of a state."

"Addict?"

"If you can call it addiction." Dan heard the puzzlement in his own voice. "It's something different, I think. More what they call psychological dependence. Perhaps it's something to do with what you were mentioning yesterday, this search for security. I had a long talk with her and asked all the questions I could think of, and she gave me much clearer answers than I was expecting. But even so I'm still sweating on what she told me."

"Such as?"

Dan ran over their conversation, frowning. "What fogs me," he finished, "is—Hmm! I was going to say her cold-blooded attitude, but that's not right. It's more her open-eyed recognition of the fact that what she's doing is dangerous."

"You find that surprising?" Redver countered curtly. "Nobody but a moron could overlook the risks, could he?"

"Is something wrong?" Dan asked in surprise, for the superintendent's voice had shaken on the last remark, and he was holding the wheel so tightly his knuckles were white. Sweat glistened on his forehead, too.

"Is that thing of yours switched on?" he demanded.

"This?" Dan flipped the lid of his stardropper. "No, of course it isn't—why?"

Then he caught on. Tilting his head, he detected at the edge of hearing a buzzing sound like a swarm of bees. But it didn't come from within the car; it was ahead of them. He said as much, and Redvers apologized with an effort.

"You're perfectly right," he said, halting the car for a stoplight. "It's that car over there—see it?"

He pointed. Slowing down on the other side of the intersection was a large Austin with a loudspeaker showing shrough the open passenger window. Once the traffic had stopped, it was plain that that was the source of the noise.

"Wired up to a stardropper?" Dan said.

"Exactly." Redvers craned to read the registration number of the offending car. "He hasn't any business to be doing that. Illegal. Noise Abatement Act."

Fumbling under the dash, he produced a microphone on a spring-loaded reel of cord and spoke briefly into it. As the lights changed to green, he put it away and let the car roll.

"They'll catch up with him in a few minutes," he said. "Though you can't help feeling sorry for the poor so-and-so—can you?"

He seemed to have recovered completely now that the noise of the loudspeaker was drowned out by the moving traffic.

"Why is he doing it?" Dan said, puzzled.

"Oh, most likely it means something to him, and he wants other people to share his so-called discovery. Or *almost* means something, and he's after someone else who can explain the rest of it. Quite common. Tell me, did Watson demonstrate his favorite setting to you, on a machine called a Gale and Welchman?"

"He did."

"Damnably attractive, isn't it? Any time you feel in danger of getting hooked yourself, call me, and I'll get one of our specialists to give you a posthypnotic against listening to stardroppers. Or was that part of your preparation for this mission? I've been told the Special Agency uses hypnosis quite a lot."

"True, it does." Dan admitted, frowning. "But—actually no. I don't suppose anybody expected it to be necessary."

"If you're lucky, it won't be," Redvers shrugged. "I can tell you personally, though, that it sometimes is. I had to have it done myself. My work was suffering. You probably noticed just now what a state I got into when that car went by."

Dan gave him a surprised glance. "Oh, you have first-hand experience, do you? I hadn't realized."

"Set a thief to catch a thief," Redvers grunted. "I didn't exactly plead to be put in charge of investigating the stardropper problem, you know. They picked on me because I was already involved."

Dan thought about that for a while, as Redvers threaded the silent little car through the dense traffic. He said at length, "So it wasn't merely the fact that I'm an Agency operative which put you on to me. It was my being an Agency operative who also happened to be carrying a stardropper."

"That's right. Not a very subtle kind of clue, hm? But don't worry—we like the Agency fine, and anyone on its staff is welcome to the free run of this tired old island. Stardroppers, on the other hand, give us nightmares. Can you wonder?"

"After what I've seen in less than twenty-four hours, no." Dan helped himself to a lighted cigarette from the dashboard dispenser; it was a brand he didn't know, British-made, and he drew on it musingly. "But it surprises me that you already have a special department to deal with this alone."

"We've grown almost paranoidally suspicious in the past ten years," Redvers sighed. "We create special departments to deal with absolutely anything that suggests it might one day lead to a major problem. Which, naturally, implies that people who picked on the wrong subject are furious when their nice private empires are hauled out from under them. . . . Sometimes I wonder whether we may not be guilty of making pessimistic prophecies fulfill themselves by giving them official recognition! But I don't think that applies in my case. Stardropping is a genuine headache for us."

"But what made you start regarding it as such—the disappearances?"

"No, not at first. It was the insanity problem, and then the question of addicition—or psychological dependence, as you prefer to call it." The words were tinged with sarcasm. "Oh, speaking of disappearances," he added, "watch your tongue with Dr. Rainshaw."

"Why?"

"His son Robin was one of the first to disappear."

Apart from the fact that the watchman at the main gate of the research station wore a gun—a rare sight in this counry where even policemen went unarmed—the establishment Dan found himself being taken to might have passed for a stately home, open to visitors at twenty-five pence a head. They were expected, and were smilingly waved through toward a wide gravel drive fringed with well-kept lawns. One of Dan's strongest impressions since coming to Britain was a sense that people here liked to take trouble over keeping up appearances—the streets were cleaner than in New York, for instance, and the grass of Hyde Park yesterday afternoon he'd found to be almost free of litter. This place was no exception. It wasn't until they'd reached a fork in the driveway and made a sharp right turn that he saw modern, single-story prefabricated buildings half-hidden among flourishing spring shrubs, identified by a sign as the scientific section of the premises. Prior to that, he'd had a fine view of a late-eighteenth-century manor house in exceptional condition, with a few cars parked in front of it.

Now, all of a sudden, he was back in modern times. He pondered this as he left the car and followed Redvers toward the nearest of the low buildings.

What, he wondered, was Rainshaw going to be like? And was it safe to ask how he felt about letting loose his discovery on the world? For good—for ill? What way was there of telling, when the same device could afflict the girl he'd seen drawing those nonsensical spirals on the pavement in Oxford Street, yet bring such a look of fulfillment to Lilith's face, like a thirsty desert traveler reaching an oasis?

Of course, as he'd been informed, Rainshaw had never claimed his discovery was other than a chance one. He had been working on the relationship between gravity and magnetism, which accounted for his having brought together a powerful magnet, a chamber containing a hard vacuum into which he was introducing counted quantities of ionized and non-ionized particles, and delicate instruments for tracking those particles, whose signals required amplification before they could be recorded.

He also had the research scientist's prime gift: a talent for seeing things when they happened, rather than what he expected to happen. Finding signals being generated in a way he could not account for, he hadn't done what the majority of people in his place might have done—shipped his equipment back to the manufacturers with a letter of complaint—but instead had followed them up, determined to isolate their cause. It was a matter of a few weeks to eliminate the nonessentials and package "the Rainshaw effect" in a box. It was a matter of months before Berghaus formulated a theory which fitted the facts, even if it didn't properly explain them. But it seemed as though it was only a matter of hours thereafter that the Rainshaw effect was forgotten and the stardropper was part of man's way of life.

Dan's first impression of the scientist was disappointing. He was a lean man, hollow-cheeked in a way which suggested he was not naturally thin but had worried himself into losing weight. He received them in an office from which a half-open door gave access to a laboratory, where a man and a girl could be seen working on a breadboard device and heard talking in low voices, and Rainshaw's eyes kept straying that way as though to make it clear he was enduring, not enjoying, the intrusion of these visitors. Having conversed politely but icily for some minutes, he contrived to impress on Dan the unmistakable impression that he tolerated such events purely because he was now a state employee, but would far rather have been free to tell them to go to hell.

Then, just as he was about ready to count the visit a waste of time, Dan happened to mention Berghaus.

Rainshaw's frozen manner changed on the instant. "You know Berghaus?" he demanded. "Were you a student of his?"

"I guess you might say so," Dan exaggerated. "Certainly he taught me what little I know about stardroppers."

"He taught all of us, including me, what we know about stardroppers," Rainshaw declared, and added in passing, "What a ridiculous name that is—don't you agree?" But his annoyance at the nickname his discovery had been afflicted with didn't wipe the new warmth form his voice. "Oh, yes—Berghaus is purely a genius! I know he maintains it was no more than a guess which led him to link his theory of precognition with my own peculiar discovery, but since then everything I've turned up, at least, can be tied neatly into his hypotheses. Oh dear! I do wish you'd mentioned this when you first came in. I must have been awfully churlish to you. But, you see, I thought I was dealing with another of this string of nosy officials who've been plaguing me for months and months." He beamed. "What precisely is it you wanted to talk to me about?"

Dan breathed a silent sigh of relief. He said, "To be candid, Doctor, I want a straight answer to a question I suspect doesn't have one. I mainly want to know whether you yourself believe these claims that have been made for stardropping—about the chance of usable knowledge being learned from listening to the machines—and, if you do take the idea seriously, whether you think the chance is good enough to justify all the suffering the habit is known to cause."

Rainshaw twisted his hands together. He said, "I sometimes wonder if I ought to feel guilty. . . . But it was pure accident, you know, and I've never claimed otherwise. So: *is* there information to be gained from stardropping? Well, Mr. Cross, all I can say is that my son—"

He broke off, and the most extraordinary expression came to his face. Dan couldn't tell whether it indicated shock, or dismay, or only a kind of weary sadness. Redvers caught his eyes and scowled, as to imply, "I warned you!"

Before Dan could frame any kind of commiserations,

though, Rainshaw recovered himself, and continued in a perfectly normal tone.

"Yes, my son thought so," he said. "And I suppose in a way he proved that he was right."

VI

The sound when Redvers exhaled in relief was like a ray of light cutting brief but alarming darkness. Dan deduced that in the past he'd had a lot of trouble from people making tactless remarks to Rainshaw. However, the scientist himself appeared not to notice. He went on talking, looking at nothing.

"Robin—well, I'd have trusted Robin's judgment as implicitly as I trust my own. He was never gullible, or easily deluded. He'd shown promise of more originality than I did at his age, and he was certainly a very dependable partner to work with. We were working together on my effect, you know, right up until the time he—ah—disappeared. And he did believe there was usable knowledge to be had from the signals."

"Where did he get this idea?" Dan ventured.

"As far as I know, it was original with himself. I've been asked, over and over"—with a faint reproving smile at Redvers—"whether he'd fallen under the influence of one of these mystical cults, but I'm certain if he had, he'd have asked what I thought about their teachings, and he never breathed a word about anything of the sort."

"Did he indicate what kind of knowledge he thought might be extracted from the signals?" Dan inquired.

"I can quote you exactly what he said, on our last evening together. We'd been arguing about this very point, and he said, 'It's so hard to capture in words—so remote from everyday experience—that I get the feeling it may really come from an alien mind.' He'd been struggling for hours to persuade me to his way of thinking, you see. It seemed actively painful for him to admit that he was failing. He even began to doubt himself, and that was why he went to his room to listen again to his big stardropper, the one he'd built himself. When I went to call him to dinner, he wasn't there. And he definitely hadn't left the house by any normal route."

Recounting incredible things, his voice was mechanical —drained of emotional judgments like belief and skepticism.

"You didn't hear anything?" Dan said. "No noise?"

Rainshaw seemed to come back to the present from a long way off. "No noise, Mr. Cross," he said heavily. "I've heard the same stories you seem to have, about people who vanished with a clap of thunder. I don't know anything about that. All I can say is my boy had gone, and he didn't leave by a door or a window. Besides, he had nothing to run away from. He was working for his doctorate and he was fascinated by his research; he was engaged to marry a charming girl. . . . No, I can only accept that he was right. He learned something from his stardropper, and the knowledge enabled him to go—elsewhere. I haven't any hope of following him. Young minds are flexible, and I'm growing old."

Like all-too-obvious background music, a spray of rain rattled at the windows and settled to a steady depressing downpour.

Accompanying Dan to the exit, Redvers set a slow pace, as though vainly hoping the rain might be over by the time they reached the outside. He said abruptly, on the point of crossing the threshold, "Remember you asked whether I really believed those stories of people disappearing?"

Dan nodded.

"I desperately want not to! But—well, I was assigned to check on Robin Rainshaw, and you've heard what his father says about his case. Faced with that kind of thing, how the hell *can* I laugh the stories off?"

"I see what you mean," Dan admitted. He had precisely the same reaction. Looking toward Redver's bright-blue car, whose top had gone up automatically at the first spatter of rain, he added, "He said he couldn't do what his son did because his mind isn't adaptable enough. Have most of the—ah—disappearers been very young?"

"Some, not all," Redvers said. He glanced at the sky.

"Come on, it's not raining that hard." But his shoes squelched in newly deep puddles as he led the way to the car. "Besides, it can't just be a question of young minds being more flexible. A hell of a lot of youngsters go insane. There hasn't been anything like it since that crazy outbreak of LSD addiction in the middle sixties. I was a brand-new detective-constable then, and I used to hate bringing those kids in—but what else could you do, when they were drooling and playing with their fingers? That, thank heaven, is over, but I'm not sure this new problem isn't even worse."

Seated at the wheel, he made no move to start the car, but sat watching raindrops trickle down the windshield.

"I can't grapple with things on this scale any longer," he said suddenly. "I'm forty-one years old, Cross, but I feel *ancient*. I just have this continual sensation that the world is shaking apart, cracking at the crust, and we're going to drop into a bottomless fissure any moment."

"We've felt that way for more than a generation," Dan reminded him.

"Oh, hell! *I* know we're lucky not to have blown ourselves up long ago! But it's one thing to be scared of what other people may do in the mass—an incompetent government, or a mob led by some hysterical rabblerouser. That's humanity, and we're stuck with it. Underneath everything you can't really think of it as alien, and I believe what's saved us for so long is the plain undeniable fact that we're all human beings. Here, though, you've got something with no precedent. Alien knowledge, they tell us. Is it? *I* don't know. But it does change people in subtle ways. You were telling me that this girl Lilith scares you because she cares so little about the risk of going crazy. That's not ordinary human, Cross. Most people would rather be dead than insane. Am I making sense, or just rambling?"

"I think you're making a lot of sense," Dan said. His mouth was very dry.

"And we can't know"—Redvers had only paused for the answer, not listened to it—"what goes on in these minds that are being changed. Not unless we get involved ourselves. I did. I found you can go so far, and then you have to make a choice: quit cold and seek help to prevent you going back, which is what I did, or decide that the rewards you can't yet understand are going to be worth more than your home, your family, your job. . . . Ah, let's go. I have work to do back in town."

He let the stored steam from earlier into the main cylinder with a faint hiss and seesawed the car out of its parking space. He didn't say anything else until they were on the road back toward central London. Then, without warning, he said, "That address your—ah—girl friend gave you. It sounded familiar. What was it again?"

Dan had memorized it; to repeat it he didn't have to consult his memo book. Redvers gave a nod.

"Yes, I place it now. It's a kind of commune, isn't it?"

"That's what Lilith said," Dan confirmed. "Why do you know about it? Have the people there given you any trouble?"

"Funnily enough, no. Apart from the fact that once a boy who was staying in the house went out of his head in the middle of the night and tried to walk off the top of the roof into midair. But they called us up at once, and—" Redvers shrugged. "That's the trouble with a bloody 'free country'! You can't do things to people for their own good! I hate to think what's becoming of the kids who are roosting there, in that high-pressure environment full of mystical nonsense, but there isn't a thing I can do to make them go home to their parents."

"Are there a lot of stardropper communes?"

"Dozens. Maybe hundreds by this time."

"And are all the people in them young?"

"Nope. I know one, so help me, which is full of lapsed Benedictine monks—broke with their Order and set up house in a derelict railway station which they bought on a mortgage. Most of them are as old as I am. But the one you're going to this afternoon is run by a fellow of—oh— twenty-four, twenty-five, name of Nicholas Carlton. Comes of a very good family. Ex-public-school prefect, captain of games, that sort of thing. Married. Wife lives there too and acts as housekeeper. There's a floating population of around a dozen, I think. But he runs it very efficiently, no doubt of that. Don't go expecting to find a kind of flophouse."

"That's interesting," Dan nodded.

"Interesting!" Redvers snorted. "I could think of another word. Carlton has intelligence and talent, and he ought to put his gifts to better use. But I'll let you form your own judgment; that's what you're here for, after all." He hesitated.

"Come to think of it," he went on, "it's a long time since I checked that place out. Must be three months at least. Do me a favor: when you leave, call me at the Yard and tell me what things are like there now."

Dan nodded. It didn't seem like too much to ask.

Glancing at the clock on the dash, Redvers said, "I'd take you to lunch out of public funds if I could, but I'm afraid I simply can't spare the time. I've been working a twelve-hour day as a matter of course recently, and I'm only scheduled for eight-plus-two. And once or twice it's gone up to fifteen."

"Don't expect me to burst out crying," Dan said wryly.

"Sorry. I deserved that. You Agency chaps are on permanent standby, aren't you?"

"Every day of the year, every hour of the day. I sometimes wonder what would happen if the world suddenly came to the boil all at once. My estimate is that I'd be working a forty-eight-hour day."

Redvers chuckled without humor. "That's an alien skill," he commented. "And if we already have people who can pull that sort of trick, why the hell anyone should bother going hunting for anything even more extraordinary beats me. . . . Well, we're getting into the middle of town. Where's the best place for me to drop you off?"

VII

Paying off his cab outside the address Lilith had given him, Dan glanced up at the house he'd been brought to. It was large, probably Victorian, in a district which he guessed would have been developed for the aspiring middle class—prosperous tradesmen and people of that kind. The tall, five-story brick buildings had mainly been subdivided, at least judging by the number of cars crammed into what had once been the front gardens but were now uniformly concrete parking areas.

This one, in particular, was very well kept, the window-frames recently painted white, the brickwork carefully re-pointed. At one of the upper windows he caught a flash of movement, and thought he recognized Lilith; she must have been watching out for him.

He walked up the path to the front door, having to thread his way between a couple of small Morrises so close together it was a wonder the driver of the second one to arrive had been able to get out when he stopped. His ringing of the bell was answered almost instantly, by a girl of twenty-five or so, not very pretty but with attractive long fair hair, wearing what had once been a red-and-white jumpsuit but was now red-and-pink after much washing.

"Yes?" she said.

"Are you—uh—Mrs. Carlton?" Dan hazarded.

"Yes," the girl confirmed. "And what—?"

She was interrupted by a shout from behind her. Lilith had made it to the first-floor landing. "It's for me, Barbie!" she called, and came down the final flight of stairs in three eager bounds. Rushing forward, she seemed to have to restrain the impulse to hug Dan.

"I thought you weren't going to come after all!" she exclaimed.

Standing aside, Barbie Carlton looked puzzled, and a trifle put out. Noticing, catching at Dan's hand to draw him inside, Lilith said, "Oh, *Barbie!* This is the guy I was expecting, the one with the American fuel-cell 'dropper!'"

Instantly Barbie showed excitement. "Ah!" she murmured, her eyes fastening hungrily on the instrument Dan carried, its strap still in a crude knot as a memorial to Lilith's unsuccessful attempt at theft. "Yes, Nick said something about that. Shall I call him? I'm sure he'd be interested."

Lilith's face fell. For her, plainly, the whole point of bringing Dan here was to have another private session with his stardropper. But it was her turn to be interrupted. A door at the far end of the hallway—giving onto a kitchen-living room, by the brief glimpse Dan had of what lay beyond—opened and revealed a young man with a shaven head, rather thin, wearing neat but old black pants and a gray shirt with the sleeves rolled up.

"Is that your American friend, Lil?" he inquired, and on Lilith's nod advanced, hand outstretched. His accent had already indicated he was probably Nicholas Carlton before he gave Dan his name.

"And you've got a Binton!" he said. "Which does something for Lil that all the other twenty-nine instruments in this house can't! It must be quite a gadget, I must say. Well, come on in. Barbie, don't let the guy stand there on the step! You've met my wife Barbara, I take it?"

During this, Dan had been taking in a series of quick impressions. They fitted what Redvers had told him. He'd been vaguely expecting something like the drug-using communes he'd occasionally visited, rather squalid, inevitably untidy, with at least the smell of decay if no actual overt garbage in the corners. This hallway, however, was starkly clean, recently painted white, and the tiled floor glistened as though it had been washed within the past hour or two. There was little furniture in sight but the hat stand—a Victorian relic—and the bookcase which he could see were well dusted, and there was a coarse Irish sisal carpet on the stairs, neatly secured by brass rods. There was a faint odor of disinfectant, piney and pleasant.

Whether or not one can tell a man by the company he keeps, Dan had long ago decided, one can certainly learn a lot about him by examining the place where he has chosen to live. At first sight, this house corresponded exactly to what Redevers had told him about Carlton; ex-prefect in an expensive boarding school. There was something school-like, or even barracks-like, about the starched inhuman, but at least it wasn't sordid.

Lilith was standing beside him quivering with impatience, and Barbie eying him with a hint of suspicion. It was time he said something, preferably affable.

"You heard how I ran into Lilith, I guess?" he said, and read from her face that she hadn't told the whole story.

"I gather you ran into her in Oxford Street, near Cosmica," Nick Carlton said, "and kindly let her try out your Binton."

"And promised to let me have another go with it today," Lilith said meaningly.

Dan chuckled. "Well, here you are!" he said, unslinging it. Continuing to Nick, he added, "I was very interested when she said she was in this—this commune, by the way. I've only just started digging around in the field, and I thought it would be worth my talking to some people who take it really seriously."

"You don't?" Nick said in surprise, and Dan saw the light of the dedicated proselytizer come into his eyes. "And yet you shelled out for a Binton? Man, either you're rolling in money or you're the kind of guy who never does anything by halves!"

Dan smiled. "Well, not the former, that's for sure. But I like to think I might be the latter. So since I'd promised Lilith she could try my instrument again, I thought I might as well take the chance of talking to the people here. If it's not an imposition."

"Imposition hell," Nick said. "I *love* talking about stardroppers." He glanced at Lilith, who was practically trembling with her eagerness to make herself scarce with Dan's instrument. "You're about to bust a gut, aren't you?" he commented. "Suppose you make it on up to your room, and I'll entertain Mr. Cross for a bit. Barbie, can you find us a drop of wine, or beer?"

"Tea or coffee," Barbie said firmly.

"Either will be fine," Dan said, realizing an answer was expected of him.

"Bless you, Nick!" Lilith exclaimed, and headed for the stairs at a dead run. Checking on the first landing, she blew Dan a kiss, and vanished. A door slammed high overhead.

"Well, come into the kitchen, then," Nick invited, and led the way. "We have to entertain visitors here, I'm afraid, because we let out all the rooms—or rather, we don't exactly *let* them. But I don't suppose I have to explain that this is a genuine commune, and we all put into it what we have to spare."

Closing the door as he waved Dan to a chair at the end of a plain wooden dining table, Barbie gave an audible snort.

"Barbara isn't quite as dedicated as I am," Nick said apologetically. "I do happen to be quite well off, actually —inherited it—and I can't think of anything better to do with what I've got than run this place. But when there isn't quite enough to go around, it's poor Barbie who has to figure out how to make ends meet. Still, she's a miracle-worker, aren't you, doll?"

Giving her an affectionate pat on the bottom as he passed, he dropped into a chair facing Dan. Meantime, she began to fill a kettle.

"So you wanted to talk to the people here," Nick resumed. "I imagine I'll probably have to do—I'm notoriously not only the most articulate but also the most loud-mouthed of the members of this little group. Also I turn off reporters very efficiently. *You're* not a reporter, are you?"

Dan shook his head, and repeated his standard cover story about how he'd been hooked by a friend recently, just before coming to London for a vacation.

"What really intrigued me," he concluded, "was being told by Lilith that only one kind of stardropper suited her. I find this hard to believe. Didn't you say you have —was it twenty-nine in this house alone?"

"Right. And all different," Nick confirmed.

"Well, if everyone here is getting *something* out of—"

"Oh, we haven't got twenty-nine people," Nick interrupted. "If that's what you're thinking. We have eleven. And they all have at least one instrument apiece, and I have six. The total is due to hit thirty in a day or two; we have someone working on a big kit-built wall-outlet unit. Show it to you later if you like—I think the guy went out for a meal."

Dan nodded. "But are all these 'droppers of different makes?" he inquired.

"Nope. Some of the manufacturers are simply in it for the money. There's a firm called Glory Joy, for instance, out in Hong Kong. If anyone offers you one of their products, drop it and run. You can't even say the repertoire of a Glory Joy stinks because it doesn't *have* a repertoire. So what we have is a selection of what we've found to be the best and most versatile instruments, and we have—oh—five or six duplicates, at least."

"But not including a Gale and Welchman?"

"Funnily enough, no. That's the one Lil keeps singing the praises of, but everyone in the house has tried a sample of it out, and nobody else gets what she got from it. You?"

"I find it the most attractive instrument I've listened to," Dan admitted after a brief pause.

"Weird," Nick said with an air of satisfaction. "Because for me it does nothing. Nothing at all."

"If Lilith gets so much out of that particular model, though," Dan suggested, "couldn't you have—well—maybe loaned her the money for a secondhand one? She was in a terrible state when I met her yesterday, and she said it was due to being without her 'dropper."

"No." The tone was final. "There's one absolutely inflexible rule about this commune of ours; regardless of what else you put into it, you *must* contribute at least one stardropper. Lilith is a special case because she would have brought hers except that her mother smashed it up. You haven't met her mother, have you? No, I suppose you couldn't have. Christ, what a nasty woman!" Nick grimaced. "So, to be perfectly candid, Lil is—ah—on probation here. We had a spare room, and we discussed it, and we decided if she was really serious about living with us she'd find the wherewithal to buy a 'dropper of her favorite make. Since we don't have one already, it would be a valuable addition to our range."

"How?" Dan countered. "By saving up out of her state unemployment benefits?" He knew she was entitled to those; anyone in Britain over the legal age to leave school was, though for people whose parents were prepared to go on accommodating them the weekly allowance was a pittance. "Or—"

He suddenly recollected what Lilith had said about doing anything he wanted her to do if he'd let her use the Binton 'dropper.

"Or going on the streets?" he finished savagely.

Neither Nick nor his wife was shocked by the accusation; instead, they were mildly amused. "You must be joking," Nick said. "What makes you think there's still money to be made on the game in this country? All the prostitutes' old customers have died off—in London, I mean. It's different in a place like—oh—Bradford."

"Or where you were at school," Barbie said. The kettle had boiled, and she was making cups of instant coffee.

Nick chuckled. "True, true! My school was allegedly very enlightened and progressive, but when it came to my trying to take a girl to bed with me in the dormitory, they drew the line. Which is how I happened to become one of the few survivors of the old guard who lost their virginity to—ah—professional therapists. Barbie's never got over that. But what the hell has this to do with what we're supposed to be talking about?"

Accepting sugar for his coffee, Dan said, "Well, I was about to ask why one has to have this vast range of different instruments, when everyone seems to settle on a personal favorite. Only we got sidetracked."

"Good question," Nick nodded. "Part of the answer is that people are different, too. My favorite isn't Barbie's, let alone that thing Lil likes so much, which I consider grossly overrated but which nonetheless is the second or third most popular brand of all. But, contrariwise, I *like* the one Barbie prefers, and I'm coming around to the suspicion that when I'm through with my current phase it may offer me something my present favorite doesn't. Are you with me?"

"One can—uh—go stale on some particular instrument?" Dan suggested.

"Oh, surely! *I* think Lilith had gone stale on her Gale and Welchman, if she got so much out of a very advanced machine like your Binton at her first attempt. Have you tried many different instruments?"

Dan shook his head. "My friend who hooked me has a Binton, and recommended it so highly I went straight for that."

"If I gave you, this minute, twice what you paid for it, would you sell it to me?" Nick inquired.

"Ah . . . I probably would," Dan conceded.

"In that case you ought to have shopped around. Bintons are very powerful—at least I've heard so; I never actually tried one. Ideally, you should be so much in love with the 'dropper you're currently using you'd rather part with your right arm. I'd let five of our six go with a smile, but the other one—*oh*, no!" He grinned engagingly. "Though ask me again in six months, and it may well be a different one I like. Let me bring in my own collection, and I'll show you some of the differences between them."

Fortunately, Dan wasn't asked outright which were his own favorites among the assorted instruments the Carltons made him experiment with. Large and heavy or small and light, plastic or wood, metal or cloth, they seemed very much alike to him, although Nick kept making such comments as "This has a magnificent repertoire!" or "I can't think what Barbie sees in this one, but she'd slaughter me if I let anything happen to it!"

Becoming much involved herself now in this display of their treasures, Barbie pulled a face at him and launched into an attempted explanation of her preference. Having found that all the noises he was invited to listen to were as enigmatic—and occasionally as unpleasant—as those he could find in his own stardropper, Dan hardly made an effort to follow her; instead, he took the chance of asking some questions that had been troubling him.

"Ah . . . does anything that you know of help in figuring out the signals?" he ventured.

"What do you mean?" countered Nick.

"Well—is there anything one can take, for example?"

"You mean drugs?" The young man tensed. "Don't let anyone kid you into trying that sort of shortcut! Most of the bad cases you see around, the nutters babbling to themselves, thought they could save trouble by like getting stoned on acid before 'dropping. We had one like that ourselves, and the poor bastard wound up falling off the roof and breaking his pelvis! Since then we've made it an inflexible rule not to let drugs in the place. Oh, I don't mean we're puritanical about it, but—well, we allow beer and wine, but no spirits; the occasional joint of regular pot, but no high-concentration hash. You get me? And that's only to unwind with, because you can get terribly tense if you're straining after a difficult set of signals. Personally, I find the best time to use a 'dropper is about an hour or two after breakfast, when I'm well rested but back in tune with waking life. On the other hand some people like it best at two in the morning, when everything around is very quiet. It's a matter of temperament, I imagine."

"Thanks for the warning," Dan murmured. There was a pause.

"By the way," Nick said with a trace of diffidence, "while it's on the premises, would you mind very much if I tried out your Binton too?"

"Sure," Dan shrugged. "Provided Lilith's through with it."

"Oh, by now she must be," Nick assured him. "We've been chatting"—he checked his watch—"Christ, nearly two hours! I'll pop up and see how she's doing. She may very well have fallen asleep, you know. Lots of people do, after a bout of intensive 'dropping. Barbie doll, fix some more coffee while I'm gone, hm?"

He left the kitchen door open behind him, and his feet could be heard on the stairs as he ran up to Lilith's room. Accepting the offer of the coffee, Dan idly inspected the stardroppers ranked on the table before him, noting the individual design variations but unable to associate them with the different signals he'd had demonstrated.

His line of thought was suddenly cut short by a cry from Nick, shouting down from the upstairs landing.

"Dan! Barbie! Lilith's gone out!"

Barbie almost dropped her kettle as she made to replace it on the stove, and rushed to the door. "Are you sure?" she called back. Following her, Dan caught her arm.

"Does he mean she made off with—?"

"With your 'droper?" By this time Nick had reached the lowest flight of stairs and was coming down them two at a time, eyes shining. "No, I have it here. But there was a note tucked in the strap—see?"

He showed the instrument to Dan. The strap was tidily wound around the case, and between two turns the corner of a sheet of paper had been slipped, bearing the single-word message "Thanks!"

Suddenly the hallway was alive with people. Every door leading onto it, and onto the upper landings, opened, and the entire commune group hurried to assemble around Dan and Nick. He heard confusing remarks he couldn't fathom—"Went out? Must have been a good one! What with? Binton! Hey do you suppose if I . . . ?"

Eventually he sorted things out. These people believed, like Dr. Rainshaw, that Lilith had been able physically and literally to vanish. There seemed to be only one sensible thing to do. While everyone else was involved in the babble of excited discussion, he slipped out of the house to find a phone booth, and from there called Redvers at the Yard.

VIII

There was a long silence after he had recounted the afternoon's events. At last the superintendent gave a heavy sigh.

"This is where it really starts, Cross. Not when a young genius like Robin Rainshaw goes out. When the word gets around that a mere schoolkid has done it—someone who most likely took up stardropping as a fad, because so many of her friends were doing it. I expect it to rain for forty days. And I don't know where the Ark is, or even if there's one being built."

The flood image was one which Dan himself had in mind already. He'd just been mentally comparing his situation with that of a man who sets out to cross an apparently level street awash with rainwater, and finds the puddles up to his waist and still rising.

Compared to other assignments he'd undertaken for the Agency, this mission had seemed petty. Granting that the discovery of a means of instantaneous displacement could entrain all the consequences he'd discussed with Redvers, he hadn't taken that aspect of the matter seriously. He'd been told to come to Britain and talk with stardropping fans, learn what he could about the rumors of researchers disappearing, but not with any expectations of confirming them—only with the intention of assessing whether the resulting social disturbance threatened to destabilize the precarious balance of world peace.

But according to what he'd been given so far—it would be an exaggeration to say "what he'd found out"—the Agency had fallen into a trap it had managed to evade for the first twelve years of its existence. It had taken for granted that something unprecedented couldn't be true. Collectively, the Agency shared Dan's original view of stardropping: just another fad, which would have its day and wane, leaving no more than a few negligible traces of its passage.

What they'd mistaken for the rumble of traffic, in other words, had proved to be the harbinger of earthquakes.

Dry-mouthed, he said to Redvers, "You don't seem to disbelieve these people's acceptance that Lilith genuinely vanished."

"I told you this morning: what Rainshaw believes, I'm driven to believe myself. You too?"

"I —I don't *want* to," Dan muttered.

"Want or not want, it doesn't make any difference. This is damned well *happening*! I appreciate your giving me an early warning of this latest case, but all I can do is drop some heavy hints to the various news media, and sooner or later hints will stop being any use. People are beginning to get scared, you know."

"Of what? Disappearing?"

"Hell, no! Someone else getting at this secret first."

"I saw two Chinese in Cosmica Limited yesterday," Dan said. "I wondered about that. Doesn't the Chinese government discourage stardropping?"

"True, but they have a crash research program staffed by brilliant university students. Didn't your briefing tell you that? I thought that point wouldn't have been overlooked. And Rainshaw is working at a state research centre here, instead of for the commercial company that used to employ him. Cross, when I told you everyone else had got into this scene ahead of the Agency, I wasn't playing with words. It's *fact*. I feel like a man trying to beat out a fire with an old dry sack, and finding sparks burning holes through every time he thinks it's smothered. Can't you imagine what'll happen the day someone really newsworthy vanishes from the plain sight of reputable witnesses? All those headlines: 'Secret lore from Aliens! Miracle talents from Stardropping!' A few thousand people will kill themselves in frustration; a few tens of thousands, already into the act, will move on to the stage of real addiction and give up caring about ordinary living; and a few *millions* will go out and buy their first stardroppers, convinced it's something they have to take seriously after all."

"Is just disappearing such a tempting thing?"

"Try looking at it less critically. Think of it as *performing a miracle*, and you'll see." There was a drumming noise from the far end of the phone line, as though Redvers was beating on his desk with bunched knuckles. "*I* don't find anything madly attractive about that kind of supernatural parlor trick, and I don't imagine you do. But because of Berghaus's theory, a lot of people will reason it this way: someone has alien talent I haven't got; someone who doesn't like me can use that talent against me; I've got to get in first! It's what the military strategists have been warning us about for years, the crucial breakthrough by one side which is likely to make the other side so desperate they'll feel compelled to hit out before they're put at a hopeless and permanent disadvantage. Cross, how soon are you going to file your first report?"

"Well—"

"I'm asking you," Redvers cut in, "to do it today. I haven't any authority for that, but . . . well, the Agency is a kind of planetary fire brigade, isn't it? And I smell smoke."

Dan thought for a long moment.

"I'll put in a report at once," he said finally. "And what's more I'm going to code it red."

"Thank God," Redvers said. "If that means anything. I used to think it did. Nowadays I'm not sure any longer."

Dan had left his Binton being passed from hand to hand among the marveling members of the stardropper commune. He didn't bother going back for it. It was expensive, and he'd be required to account for its loss, but right now, he'd as soon have gone to take back a bagful of rattlesnakes.

The report he planned to file could be turned in over an ordinary phone circuit; however, there were good reasons for preferring privacy at the speaking end of the connection, and since Redver's men had already checked his hotel room for bugs, he headed straight back there. He was given a clear transatlantic satellite connection very quickly, it being by now after business hours in London, and shortly heard a familiar recorded voice inviting him to go ahead, followed by the three shrill pips which were a key to his personal code. He closed his eyes.

"Oh-four," he said. "Equanimity is inversely by the clyster. When it was in the trivial four-by-four the virtue was imported, but the wall fell between the crackle and the potiphar. . ."

It was a curious uplifting sensation to hear himself speak this way, perhaps akin to the transcendental insight some people claimed to achieve through drugs or starvation or delirium. During his first two years with the Agency, he had undergone a complete course of analysis conducted by a specially trained neo-Freudian. From the complex personal associations revealed by the analysis they had built up a word-for-word code covering the equivalent of a good-sized desk dictionary. New words and personal names could be spelled out; for every letter of the alphabet and for every number up to a hundred there were a dozen associated phrases. Next he had been made to learn the code, pumped into him under deep hypnosis. The Agency used hypnosis a great deal, having refined the traditional techniques with the aid of drugs.

The memorizing had taken a mere three months. Now, at the Agency's main office in New York, there was a computer—number 04—into which they would feed the tape bearing his report, and it would print out in clear.

The method wasn't perfect. It was fat, to begin with, running a minimum twenty percent longer than clear language and occasionally as much as sixty percent, and sometimes sentence structure survived the coding procedure. But because the equivalence depended on Dan's personal memories and not on a process that could be attacked statistically it would probably take longer to break than it had taken to build up. Even Dan himself could not decipher a transcript of one of his own reports; it required a post-hypnotic trigger, such as the three pips he'd heard on the phone this time, to make the code accessible to his conscious mind.

Four pips on a lower tone followed his signing off, and he instantly forgot again how to speak in the code. His sense of elation lingered, though. It was sometimes very strong, as he imagined the aftermath of a vision might be to a mystic—a feeling that he had been briefly in closer touch with reality. He'd asked the analyst who had laid the foundations for the code about this, and had been told that in fact there was a more mundane explanation. Most people, the analyst asserted, had the ability to recall in the proper context a word they hadn't thought of for years, even decades: perhaps a technical term, perhaps a foreign name. Given the right stimulus, up it would pop. And this of itself usually made the person affected feel pleased. In the case of an Agency code, there was a reinforcement. Ordinary language was a series of labels invented by other people; Agency codes were derived from remembered events that were exclusively significant to the user, so recovering the knowledge of them and knowing them to have been usefully employed was a little like the case of a composer, say, who while walking down the street heard other people, total strangers, humming a song he had made up so long ago he'd almost forgotten about it.

Whatever explanation might account for the experience, it was a valid one. Dan felt like a cat full of cream as he lounged in his armchair after completing his report. It wasn't until, feeling for his cigarettes, he discovered a slip of paper in his pocket that he snapped back into contact with reality.

He'd abandoned his stardropper at the Carlton's commune. But he'd claimed the note Lilith had left, with its single scribbled word bold and black on the narrow white page.

Had she slipped away like a mouse into a hole, wanting perfect privacy for some reason of her own? Or had she gone as Dr. Rainshaw alleged his son had gone—"miraculously"? If so, should he pity her?

Or envy her?

Which?

IX

Through the main bar of the Hunting Horn pub, up a flight of stairs, he reached the meetingplace of the Club Cosmica. At the head of the stairs a girl volunteer was taking admission fees—a student, by the look of her. She was furnished with a list of recognized guests on which she found his name, and waved him by without charging anything.

He passed on into a large room, divided by a heavy curtain three-quarters drawn into a meeting hall with rows of chairs facing a dais and a kind of antechamber where there was a bar. It was still nearly twenty minutes before the advertised time of starting, but already there were some forty people standing around in knots of four to six.

The people he'd met at the commune this afternoon had been—congruous? Was there such a word? The hell with it. They fitted. He recalled Redver's wry joke about "star-dropping out." The members of the commune were the Carltons' age or younger, clean but shabbily dressed, with the indefinable stamp of the social rebel. Here, in utter contrast, the atmosphere was that of a heavily patronized bar in some prosperous business district: the men wore well-tailored suits, the women and girls had fashionable outfits and expensive coiffures, not to mention jewelry restrained enough to be very valuable. And they were drinking vodkatinis or dry sherry.

The sheer paradox of it confused him terribly. When else in all of history had people joined smart social clubs to meddle with something equally dangerous?

Oh, maybe in ancient China they had fireworks parties and amused themselves elegantly with that newly discovered substance, gunpowder!

Affable, Watson spotted him and came over to greet

him. Having bought him a drink, he invited him to meet some of the members. As he was piloted from group to group, Dan caught snatches of conversation, but like the articles in the hobby magazines he'd read, it all seemed dismayingly remote from the reality of a girl who had vanished from her tiny attic room, or a father mourning the loss of a son he did not believe dead yet never expected to see again.

"—but the whole question of subjective-objective comes in here, so let's not get metaphysical. Objective so far as we are concerned means you can make it do things. Postulate a field such that—"

"—concede that an installation like his certainly uses a lot of power, but where's the benefit in that? Anyone could hook a 'dropper on a thirty-two-thousand-volt power cable and the signals would be heard from here to Yucatan, but it's a waste of effort, *I* think—"

Those speakers were both serious, intense young men, illustrating their points with slipsticks. Others were struggling, their eyes haunted, to get across meanings they were convinced no words could properly express. They seemed infinitely distant from anything Dan had encountered in other contexts.

"—nature of the signal in Berghaus's view. I mean, identity of function isn't identity of nature. Department of truisms now open." This was a man of about thirty in an old suit, his hair rumpled, his eyes fierce and bright behind strong glasses. "To say this is what the signals are *like* tells you precisely nothing. Any day now someone may work up an explanation without reference to psychic continua at all."

On his left a girl with shoulder-length fair hair, dressed in lounging culottes and a fashionable tunic of imitation feathers, gave a slow headshake. "I think you should try being a bit more humble, Jerry. To my mind the first thing the signals convey is what they are. Just by listening you get this instinctive sense you're eavesdropping on the minds of the universe at work."

"Maybe it does to you, Angel. To me it says nothing of the kind. You're just oversusceptible. Your imagination was caught by Berghaus's idea, and bang! It was revealed truth."

The girl he had called Angel raised one eyebrow. She was very pretty, but her face was drawn and tired. She said, "Well, well! Jerry Berghaus plus, I presume! You know as well as I do that Berghaus approached the matter with an open mind—"

"And leapt miles ahead of any objective evidence!" snapped Jerry.

"Because he experienced for himself the self-identifying information in stardropper signals!" the girl flared.

Watson excused himself to Dan in a whisper and went through to the other half of the hall; there were some sort of preparations going on the dais, presumably for the promised demonstration.

"Look," the man Jerry said with careful patience, "no one disputes that Berghaus accounted neatly for precognition. What I'm saying is that when he came to stardropping he applied Occam's razor needlessly and stretched his precog theory to include that too simply because of the one factor they had in common: neither could be explained in traditional terms."

A lean, fiftyish man on the other side of Angel took a pipe from his mouth and frowned. "But is Berghaus what you'd call an enthusiast?" he said. "I gather he's not."

"He told me—" Dan said, and broke off, because instantly all the eyes of the group were on him. Well, it was a fast way of staking his claim in the conversation. "He told me he thought that if the signals are of alien origin they'll probably be intrinsically incomprehensible."

"You know Berghaus?" Angel said in a wondering voice.

"Well, I've met him and talked about this to him."

"And that louse Wally Watson didn't bother to mention it to us?"

"I don't think I told him," Dan said. He felt the mood of the group shift toward awe: *here's a man who knows Berghaus and is modest about it!* All the dogmatism went out of Jerry. He spoke in a changed voice.

"Well—uh—I'm Jerry Bartlett, and this is Angel Allen. And Leon Patrick," the man with the pipe offered his hand for a foursquare shake. "And . . ."

The other two in the group muttered names Dan barely heard; they both seemed to be listeners, not talkers. Angel kept her eyes on his face.

"But he must take his theory seriously," she insisted.

"I assume he does. But he certainly doesn't pin as much faith to it as most people seem to."

"So much for your 'self-identifying' bit," Jerry said to Angel.

"Not at all." She rounded on him sharply. "Can you tell me how it feels to ride a bicycle?"

"Don't be irrelevant. You sit astride it, you put one foot—"

"I didn't ask you to explain the mechanics of it. I said tell me how it feels. You can't verbalize the balancing sensation you experience. But you can learn it when it happen to you. Human beings *can* absorb nonverbal knowledge. We just aren't very good at it."

"You're not falling for this supernatural-wisdom bit, are you?" Jerry's bluster was beginning to return.

"If you've started to resort to loaded words like 'supernatural,' it seems to me you're afraid of being convinced. In which case, what the hell are you doing here?"

"I'm a physicist. Stardropper signals are a phenomenon in my province, obviously. What annoys me is people like you telling me I ought to be humble—when did *I* claim to know more than Berghaus?"

Angel sighed. "What gives you the impression that *I* did? All I'm saying is that he proposed his theory because the signals convey a hint of their own nature, which I've experienced myself. If Berghaus does have reservations, that's what I've always been taught to regard as a proper scientific attitude. Now let's hear your reasons for contesting *that*!"

Before Jerry could utter his counterblast, plainly boiling at the tip of his tongue, they were interrupted by Watson's voice calling them to take their places for the demonstration, and they joined a slow shuffling procession into the other half of the room. Dan hoped the argument might resume later. There was something reassuring about the fact that some people at least were approaching the subject from this highly critical standpoint, instead of simply swallowing Berghaus's theory whole in the manner displayed by the members of the Carlton's commune.

At Angel's invitation, he took a place in the front row

between her and the pipe-smoking Leon Patrick. On the dais stood a huge stardropper on a rubber-tired trolley, attended by Watson and a roly-poly man in shiny-seated slacks and a green sweater; while Watson made delicate adjustments to its controls, the latter was listening intently through earphones, gesturing vigorously.

The adjustments satisfactorily completed and the audience settled down, Watson called the meeting to order and read a set of formal minutes, which were largely concerned with routine matters such as raising the membership fee and organizing a charter flight for members of the club to attend a stardropping congress in Oslo. Then he called for a report from the membership secretary, a drab woman of young middle age, noticeably worse-clad than most other people here, about whom the only touch of color was her hair—faded carroty-red, and probably dyed. Dan gathered that her name was Mrs. Towler.

But he didn't pay much attention to these proceedings; they seemed appallingly banal.

Eventually, however, all that was disposed of, and Watson rose again to introduce their guest speaker for the evening: the roly-poly man, whom he presented as Dr. Jock Neill from the University of Strathbran in Scotland.

Neill was very excitable; he talked fast, with a great deal of jargon, and what was worse from Dan's point of view with a ferocious Scots accent. After the first few minutes it hardly seemed worth trying to follow his discourse in detail; accordingly he let his mind drift back to the line of argument Angel and Jerry had been pursuing.

The girl's contention that the signals were self-identifying was as useful a piece of logic as a medieval schoolman's. If you didn't accept the postulate, it fell down; if you did, it was a perfect defense against any contrary assertion. She seemed to have accepted it *in toto*. Did her obvious tiredness indicate that she was in an obsession-state akin to Lilith's, and merely better equipped than a simple schoolgirl to put her opinions into convincing words? There was no way, as yet, that Dan could tell, but he made a mental note to engage her in further conversation.

It would be very reassuring to find that in some cases,

at least, stardropper "addiction" could co-exist with enduring rationality.

Was Jerry an example of that? Dan rather thought not. He was such a contrast with Angel. Clearly he was a skeptic, waiting for the evidence of some special personal experience before conceding that there were truths not accounted for in his scientific canon. He had said he was a physicist, investigating a phenomenon in his own province, but on the basis of what he'd been told in his briefing, let alone what he had more recently learned, Dan would have been prepared to argue the contrary. Even Berghaus agreed that a stardropper transcended orthodox physics. That might well be what was making Jerry so dogmatic and aggressive—the suspicion that his cherished beliefs were about to be overturned.

A painful process!

Neill reached the end of his exposition, to the relief of some people in the audience who had apparently lost track in the same way as Dan, and the lights went down and the demonstration began. From a speaker hung on the side of the stardropper trolley there swelled a vast busy noise suggesting a factory, or perhaps a whole industrial town. Having spared it his full concentration for a minute or two, Dan decided it was just a noise as far as he was concerned, and reverted to wrestling with his own complex thoughts.

One thing was clear: not everyone gave credit to the notion that stardropping was a key to mystic alien knowledge. Jerry had specifically pooh-poohed the idea. And this man beside him, Leon Patrick, formal of manner and well past the excitable age, had seemed to incline to the same view. Dan marked him down also on the list of people he wanted to have another talk with; one would assume him to be a successful business executive—not, *a priori*, a very credulous type.

There was a tremendous racket coming from the loudspeaker now. It kept driving his thoughts into channels he didn't want them to wander down, but perfect concentration was out of the question. He recalled the snatch of conversation he had overheard about an installation which used a lot of power. Could the equipment referred to have been Neill's? If so, what benefit might the extra power offer? Granting Berghaus's hypothesis of a non-Einsteinian continuum, was there a linear relationship between power and range in the case of a stardropper? If there were, it followed that increasing the power would defeat the object of the exercise. The more power you used, the lower would be the chance of receiving signals from one single source, into which the linearly organized human brain might conceivably read a clear meaning without distraction, and the greater the risk of picking up two, ten, or a thousand signals overlaid one on top of the other. Therefore the optimum approach should lie in employing the minimum quantity of power, to reduce equipment noise, and ...

He was beginning to feel giddy. He had a curious sense of frustration, as though he had a word on the tip of his tongue, due to contemplating the improbability of a linear power-range relation in a Berghausian continuum. Given that this was a genuine problem, however, that didn't mean it was insoluble. As Jerry had rightly said, identity of function isn't identity of nature, and the fact that stardropper signals were conveniently presented through an earpiece was due to an accidental human predisposition. Words and mathematical symbols and variables in an analog computer went through the same motions as their real-world counterparts and were not those counterparts. The resemblance between a stardropper and a portable radio was coincidence. If some brand-new mode of conveying the information had been adopted, such as direct input through the skin, would ... ?

With an effort as tremendous as heaving up a gigantic weight, Dan seized control of his mind. He had had a momentary impression that he was thinking in several directions at once, his consciousness ballooning out from a center. It was one of the most shocking sensations he had ever experienced.

For a few seconds he remembered where he was and what was going on, and heard the sound the stardropper on the dais was now emitting; a liquid pulsating noise with a definite but irregular rhythm, like bubbles coming to the surface of a pan of boiling water. Then he felt himself tugged back into his stream of speculation.

Look: it *couldn't* be that a big, power-hungry stardropper had a greater "range," because the whole point about Berghaus's new kind of continuum—invented to account for information transfer future-to-past—was that within it distance, in the normal sense of space-covered-in-measured-time, was theorized out of existence.

But, if you discarded distance, how could you have separation? How could there be discrete—anythings?

Easily, of course. That was the truly astonishing thing. Hadn't events been turned up by nuclear physicists which called for precisely that? Like an electron departing simultaneously in more than one direction from a given point, or coexisting with itself on two different paths. There was your separation, and there was your absence-of-conventional-distance. Because the *one* electron involved wasn't traversing an intervening space. The whole point of Berghaus's hypothesis was that in his continuum "instantaneity" had to reacquire the meaning it had lost in Einstein's, where it takes time for even a beam of light to cover the gap between source and recipient.

You could justifiably say, in that case, "at the same time." Which you couldn't in Einsteinian terms.

But that meant—!

He was never so angry in his life as he was for the next few moments. On the brink of fitting together his newly formulated thoughts about the nature of things in this eerie alternative kind of space Berghaus had postulated, he was slammed back to the here-and-now, back to the room over the pub, back to the distractions of sensory input. Choking with rage, he opened his eyes.

Fractionally afterward the lights went up, and his fury was displaced by amazement. What in hell was he doing sprawled idiotically sideways across the chair next to his own? The noise of the stardropper ceased abruptly. There was a shrill cry in a girl's voice, and a wave of frightened exclamations followed.

"Leon!" someone said clearly. "Where's Leon?"

Dan pushed himself back to an upright position and remembered that the chair alongside his had been Leon Patrick's. The chair was empty, and across it Angel was staring at him with naked terror in her eyes.

He rose slowly to his feet. Neill and Watson were hurrying down from the dais, the former gesticulating wildly, the latter solemnly calm. Everyone fell silent, as though confident Watson would give them a lead.

"You were thrown across Leon's chair, weren't you?" Watson said to Dan, raising his voice so that all present could hear him.

"Yes!" Dan felt his palms sticky with sweat.

"And there was a slamming sound—like a gigantic handclap?"

A dozen eager voices confirmed this.

"Then," Watson said after a pause, "I'm afraid we may have seen the last of Leon Patrick."

He hesitated while a wave of horror and dismay went through the audience, and finished, "Poor devil!"

X

Dan remembered clearly when he had last seen so many ghastly-white faces at once: at the scene of a collision where a bus had slammed into a station wagon with four kids in the back and killed them all. And it wasn't just the paleness that was the same. There were the same expressions, too—the look of people reminded in a flash that they were involved in a dangerous pursuit.

And who had, until this moment, shared the attitude Lilith had invoked to explain why she wasn't concerned about the risk of going insane. This sort of thing "happened to someone else."

It was pitiable to watch them struggling to adjust—not that Dan had much attention to spare from his own chaotic thoughts. "Someone tell his wife?" came a nervous half-question from a man Dan hadn't met, and Watson gave a nod.

"I'll take care of that. Don't worry."

Upon which the assembly started to disperse, leaving Dan baffled. Surely this couldn't be the limit of their reaction—the snuffing out of a life glossed over as lightly as the extinction of a candle flame? But no one else seemed to question that Patrick's vanishing was simply an event to be accepted. The slamming noise apparently indicated that something had gone wrong. Too bad!

Helpless, he looked around for guidance. The girl Angel was staring at Leon's chair, her cheeks pale, her lower lip caught between her teeth; she was hugging her arms close to herself as though to control a fit of shivering. Neill, his face lugubrious, had turned back to the dais to disconnect his machine. That left Watson, impassive as a statue of Buddha.

"But"—Dan hadn't meant to speak; the words came of their own accord. "But aren't you going to . . . ?"

"What, Mr. Cross?" Watson returned.

"Well—call the police, or something!"

"And what crime is supposed to have been committed?" Watson snapped crushingly. Raising his voice, he added, "This meeting is declared closed!"

"No! Oh, *no!*"

The cry was flung like a bomb, and everyone still in the room turned to stare at the speaker. It was the membership secretary, Mrs. Towler, elbowing her way through those trying to leave in order to confront Watson.

"No, that's not fair!" she went on, aggressive now she was the center of attention. Dan saw a trembling of her mouth that suggested she might burst out crying. "I was getting something, I swear I was, and it's the first time I ever did, and I don't see why I should be cheated like this!"

"Ghoul!" a voice said at Dan's elbow, barely above a whisper. He jerked his head around to discover that it was Angel who had addressed him.

"What?"

"I said 'ghoul'! Can you imagine anything nastier than wanting to go on after—?" She gestured at the chair which had been Patrick's, and added with a bitter smile, "Shall we leave them to fight it out? Or are you in the ghoul line too?"

For a moment, to his own dismay, Dan found himself hesitating. He recalled that he also had been on the verge of some revelation, and that he had been angry when it was snatched from him. But it was no more real to him now than a dream, or the transitory euphoria which followed the use of his personal spoken code.

"Let's get the hell out," he said. "I imagine you could use a drink, and I'm damned sure I could."

The downstairs bar was already crowded with the members of the club, being interrogated by the ordinary customers about why they were so upset. Dan sent Angel to a corner table that was still vacant and somehow contrived to avoid being questioned himself while he was collecting double Scotches for them both. Others, Jerry Bartlett among them, had not been so lucky, and there was a buzz of muted alarm in the air.

Yet . . .

He shook his head in incredulity. Redvers had hit on the right point when he said, "Try thinking of it as 'performing a miracle.'" Yet these people didn't react as though they'd been present when a miracle happened. It might have been nothing more than—than, say, the breaking of a storm, which was now offending the ear with dismal rain.

In the case of those who hadn't been upstairs, that was predictable. But in the case of those who had . . .

He sat down beside Angel, handed her her drink, and offered cigarettes. Taking one, she gave a sudden harsh laugh.

"It's different actually being there when it happens, isn't it? I'm sort of having to rearrange my private universe."

Noticing that his hand shook visibly when he held his lighter out, Dan said, "Didn't you believe it was true?"

"Oh, I believed it in my mind." Breathing smoke, Angel leaned back with a mutter of thanks. "I had to. After all, I was engaged to Robin Rainshaw. But I didn't believe it in my guts, where it matters."

"*You* were Robin Rainshaw's fiancée?" Dan halted the lighter in midmovement so abruptly the flame blew out.

"I was. Am, I suppose, failing his return to collect this." She turned a ring on her finger which he hadn't noticed. "But you sound as though you knew him. Did you?"

There was a pleading note in the words, but wistful, as though she was prepared to be disappointed. He disappointed her.

"I'm afraid not. I only heard about him."

"Not many people even heard." Angel moved her glass on the table between them as on a chessboard—a knight's move, with the unique diagonal kink in the middle of it. And fell silent, though Dan had expected her to continue.

His hand still trembling, he finally got his own cigarette lit, and said when he was sure Angel didn't propose to add anything, "You know what beats me?"

"Probably the same that beats me. But go ahead anyway."

"The—the way all these people are shrugging it off! As

though there wasn't anything extraordinary about a man disappearing into thin air!"

She gave him a curious look. "You're a real novice, aren't you?" she said. "In spite of claiming to know Berghaus, and being so well informed in so many ways."

"Yes—hell! I *am* a novice, I guess. But how do people stop being novices if they won't learn by asking questions?"

"In this business you don't learn by asking. You only learn by experience."

"But if you're apt to vanish in a clap of thunder, what in hell can induce anyone to want more—*experience?*"

Before Angel could reply, there was a distraction. The red-haired Mrs. Towler rushed down the stairs from the clubroom and forced a path to the street door, tears streaming down her face. A murmur of incredulous comment followed her.

In her wake Watson appeared, his face tired and pale. He stood watching until Mrs. Towler had gone out, then collected himself a drink at the bar and glanced around. Spotting a vacant chair at the table Dan and Angel were using, he sat down unbidden.

"Did you cool her down?" Angel asked, with a headshake toward the door through which the weeping woman had left.

"Sort of. I promised her a private session with Jock Neill's equipment. It was all I could think of."

"She isn't going to make it, though, is she? Regardless of what anyone does for her." Angel didn't look at him as she posed the question.

"I wouldn't care to make a prophecy about that," Watson said wryly as he sipped his drink. "She might. Though, admittedly, if she does she's likely to go out like Leon."

"Do you think *I'll* ever make it?" Now Angel raised her head and stared him straight in the face.

"I'm not going to risk predictions about anyone," Watson muttered. "You just keep trying until something happens."

Carefully choosing the nastiest available turn of phrase, Dan cut in. "It seems to me that people who want to carry on when they have an example like Patrick before them have a lot in common with drug addicts, going on doping when they know what's in store."

He had intended the remark to be provocative. He

wasn't prepared for the raw fury which blazed in Angel's eyes, nor for her to thrust back her chair as though to storm away in disgust. But Watson, though he whitened around the lips and eyes, controlled himself and caught her by the arm, making her sit down again by main force.

"I don't know what you expect to gain by that cheap kind of baiting, Cross," he said tightly. "But I'll accept that you've had a shock. All of us have. There's no need, though, to fling insults around."

Dan muttered something inaudible; even he wasn't certain what he'd had in mind.

"Do I look like a dope peddler?" Watson pursued.

"Do they ever?" Dan snapped.

Watson flushed. He said, "Is that all you think stardropping amounts to—an escape from reality, like drugs? Well, it's the exact fucking opposite!" He slammed his balled fist on the table, making their glasses jump. Now it was Angel's turn to try and calm him down, but he shook her hand off and leaned close to Dan, his voice tremulous with conviction.

"Stardropping is quite literally what Berghaus guessed it might be—a path to new knowledge! But to grasp it requires an act of mental agility you can only compare to making a great scientific discovery. And when in all of history has the chance been offered to everyone, every single member of the human race, to share in that kind of experience? Hm?"

"But—" Dan began, and was cut short.

"If you're not interested in the offer that's being made, then the hell with you!" Watson seized his glass and drained it at one draught. "Go give that pretty Binton of yours to someone who cares, someone who thinks it's *important* to bust down the blind blank walls of stale tradition and open his mind to new data, new discoveries new achievement! Stay in your mud-wallow and be happy if you prefer, but don't pester *me* with your stupid insults!"

There was a pause, which happened to coincide with a general silence into which one of the barmaids threw a shrill insincere laugh. Watson's tension subsided. He said as the regular babble of conversation resumed, "Sorry. It's been a shock to us all, as I said. Leon was a long-time member of the club, and . . . Another? What was it?"

Dan would have preferred to get away from the pub altogether, but duty impelled him to carry on until he couldn't stand the pressure a moment longer. He accepted the offer, and sat silently with Angel until Watson returned from the bar with the refilled glasses.

"Cheers," he said, sitting down again. "Sorry, Cross. I didn't have to blow my top any more than I said you did. Let me tell you a little story which I just remembered. Once a European found himself among a people so primitive they hadn't invented the wheel. He decided to show them how to make carts and lighten their work.

"Well, at first they were delighted. But then the day came when one of the carts overturned, and the natives saw one of the wheels spinning around on its axle in midair. And they took to their heels, and from that day forth they'd have nothing to do with the carts. A wheel rolling along the ground—that was all right. But one spinning of its own accord in the air smacked of magic, and they were terrified."

"Don't tell me you're the missionary teaching us about the wheel!" Dan said acidly.

"No, but Berghaus is—even though he may well not realize it himself."

"What makes you so sure?" Dan challenged. "Have you made some fantastic discovery through your 'dropper, or are you indulging in wishful thinking like Mrs. Towler?"

"I thought we had given up needling each other," Watson said in a tone of mild reproof. "Anyway, what answer would you expect to that question? If I say yes, you'll say, 'Show me! Teach me!' And that's impossible. But if I say no, you'll ask why I'm so sure there is this new knowledge to be had."

Dan hesitated, seeking a line of approach that might breach that all-too-logical defense. He said finally, "Well, something obviously happened to Leon Patrick. Do you claim to know what it was?"

Watson took his time over replying, his eyes—very bright —fixed on Dan's face. He said at last, "Frankly, Mr. Cross, I think you're a sensation-seeker rather than a serious researcher, but I'll give you the same answer anyhow because I think Angel might understand it even if you don't."

"So you think you *can* explain what became of Patrick!" Dan snapped, nettled.

"I didn't say that. I can *tell* you what happened to him; *explaining* it is something else." Watson sipped his drink and wiped his lip with the back of his hand. "Quite simply, Leon learned something. But he didn't get the whole of it. Tell me, have you ever dropped an old-fashioned light bulb, the kind called vacuum-filled?"

"I don't think I—oh! The sound?"

"That's right."

Angel was looking from one to other of them, mystified. "Light bulb?" she echoed, puzzled.

"If someone did physically vanish, there would be an implosion. And a sound like a thunderclap. Displaced air rushing into vacancy." Dan felt his nape prickle. This was logical, where so many other aspects of the matter had been crazy. He went on, turning to her, "There was no sound when your friend Robin disappeared, was there? Watson, suppose Patrick had vanished silently?"

"He would answer to 'Hi!'," said Angel, and laughed.

"What?"

"Carroll. *The Hunting of the Snark*. When the snark proved to be a boojum he softly and silently vanished away." Angel gulped the rest of her drink and rose. "Sorry. I'd better do exactly that myself. I'm a bit hysterical."

"Shall I run you back?" Watson offered. "You live around the corned from Cosmica, don't you?"

"Thanks, I have my own car. You stay and answer some more of Dan's questions. He needs his hand held. He's scared."

With quick irregular steps she went to the street door. As she passed, Jerry Bartlett called after her, but she ignored him. He looked around, caught sight of Watson, and hastened over.

"I didn't see you hidden in this corner," he said. "Wally, I want to talk about Leon. Can I join you?"

He sat down without waiting for an answer, and Dan had to give up hope of continuing with his own questions as he began to speak with machinegun rapidity.

"I don't mind telling you this thing has blown my mind —absolutely blown my mind! I've never before been present when somebody went out, of course, and I wasn't entirely convinced it really happened. Now I've witnessed it myself, I'm spinning so fast I'm dizzy. I've been talking with Jock, who hadn't seen it before either, and he fetched up against the same problem I did. We can't work out the conditions for instantaneous displacement. I mean, it must be instantaneous! If a man-size body were to leave at finite speed the shockwave would probably bring the building down! All we got was this bang consistent with air imploding into a sudden void."

"If you spent more time with your 'dropper and less time playing with words, Jerry, I think you might make it yourself," Watson said.

Jerry didn't seem to hear. He went on, "Now if Berghaus is right, it figures that the loudest signals on the 'dropper should be from the most highly evolved and most actively conscious species, right? So what's human evolution? Basically a story of learning to impose a desired form on environment, right? But not just physical environment: also the sequence of events experienced. The more man evolves, the more he consciously plans ahead and—uh—manipulates randomness, trying to ensure that future experiences are desirable ones. But there's a gap here, and I can't fill it in." He broke off, looking unhappy.

"Jerry," Watson said again, and this time made the words sound more like an order than a piece of advice, "you need to spend more time with your 'dropper and less time talking."

Acquiescently, Jerry got up and wandered away, lost in thought. Dan stared at Watson.

"You're a lot more than a store manager, aren't you?" he said. "These people treat you like a guru—a bonze."

"Do they?" Watson countered in a casual tone. "Well, can you think of a better niche in a commercial society for someone who's concerned to propagate knowledge he considers important?"

"Dangerous knowledge!"

"So tell me what makes knowledge dangerous. Which seems more innocuous, in your view—to teach a man to read and write, or to make gunpowder? Yet more revolutions have been carried through with literacy than with shot and shell."

He stood up. "Well, you've had a very eventful first

visit to our club, haven't you? Can I give you a lift home? I have the penthouse apartment over Cosmica Limited, if that's anywhere in your direction."

"No. No thank you. I'm going to walk. I think I need the night air to calm me down." Dan heard his own voice tinged with bitterness. "But can't you think of a stronger term to describe what's happened than 'eventful'?"

Watson fixed him with steely eyes. "I'm not callous, Mr. Cross. Leon was a good man, and I liked him. I simply have to face the fact that he wasn't *better*. Good night."

XI

The phone in Dan's hotel room rang at eight-thirty. He had slept very badly, and his eyes were stinging. He'd intended to try and doze for another hour, but it seemed like a waste of effort.

"Yes?" he said to the phone, half expecting the caller to be Redvers.

"Reception, Mr. Cross. A gentleman has left a package for you. It's a Mr. Carlton, I think. He said you'd probably want it straight away, so I hope I haven't disturbed you unnecessarily."

"No, that's all right," Dan said tiredly. "It's about the size and shape of a stardropper, is it?"

"I imagine so, sir," the reception clerk said. "But it's wrapped in brown paper."

Dan thought for a moment. The events of last evening had haunted him night-long, and he was aware of a need for ordinary human company. He said at length, "Okay, I'm planning to come down for breakfast in the lounge—I'll pick the thing up on my way past. In about twenty minutes, I guess."

The reception clerk sounded embarrassed when he answered. "Ah—I sould advise against calling at the desk, sir."

"What? Why?"

"Well, sir, we're besieged by reporters. It appears that you were involved in something yesterday which has attracted a great deal of public interest."

"Oh my God," Dan said. He sat up and reached for a cigarette. "Can't you tell them to go to hell?"

"Well, sir, we do our best to protect the privacy of our guests, but . . . Look, suppose I send up the morning papers. I think that might clarify matters."

"Yes, that's a good idea," Dan said, and added, "By the way, did you mean you'd rather not have me take breakfast downstairs?"

Slightly shocked, the clerk said, "Not at all, sir. Please do precisely as you wish. We for our part will do our utmost to ensure that no one disturbs you without your permission."

"That sounds like service," Dan grunted, and cut the connection.

He was in the shower when the bellboy brought up the promised papers, and shouted that the man should come back for his tip later. But the answer, in an offhand voice, was, "That's all right, sir. Any time!"

When he emerged from the bathroom he discovered why. All of a sudden he was in the worst possible predicament for an Agency operative. He was a celebrity. From all the papers huge blue-and-red headlines shrieked: STARDROPPER FAN VANISHES! DISAPPEARANCE OF WELL-KNOWN CITY PERSONALITY. REMARKABLE EVENT AT "STARDROPPER" CLUB. IT IS TRUE ABOUT STARDROPPING! (IS IT?)

"Christ," he said aloud, and folded the papers under his arm. Before tackling the full texts, he needed something to clear his head.

When he came out of the elevator in the foyer, he found the reception clerk hadn't been exaggerating to say that the desk was being besieged. At least thirty people were milling around in the hallway, many armed with portable recorders, and there were two TV camera teams as well. Fortunately none of them glanced his way as he hurried past and into the breakfast lounge.

Feeling as though he had just won some sort of petty victory, he sat down at a vacant table, spreading the papers out, and said to the waiter hovering beside him, "Coffee. Black. A lot of it, and quickly."

"Yes, sir," the man said, and added softly, "You are Mr. Cross, aren't you? Because the manager said that if you came down we were to ask you if you're willing to talk to those reporters out there."

"Tell the manager that as far as I'm concerned they can go jump in the Serpentine," Dan grunted. "And I'd appreciate them being kept well away from me, at least until I've had breakfast."

"We'll do our best, sir," the waiter said, though not very optimistically. "And what can I bring you anyway? Smoked haddock, ham and eggs, vegetarian savory—?"

"Just the coffee for now. I'll decide about the rest later."

"Very good, sir."

Now that was what you might call service, Dan thought as he set to studying the papers in detail. It was clear from the start that this was what Redvers had been so afraid of —the disappearance of someone newsworthy. For Patrick, it seemed, had been a director of a nationally famous real estate agency, and his son was a champion glider pilot.

He had a sickening sensation that he was sliding helplessly toward disaster.

The press had been quick, and thorough. They had got hold—by the look of it—of a membership list for Club Cosmica, and they'd tracked down Jerry Bartlett, Watson, and Angel Allen. No paper had comments from all three, but they had all got hold of at least one of the trio and one or more of the other club members. Doubtless it had taken them until this morning to locate himself only because he'd been a visitor, not a regular.

So the accolade of press authority had finally been given to all those long-stifled rumors. Now anything could happen.

Worse yet, someone had been digging in the morgue and had uncovered the human-interest angle of Angel's engagement to Robin Rainshaw. Clearly Redvers—or possibly his father—had planted a story to cover up his disappearance, and it had been accepted without question until now. Some reporter, however, had put one and two together and made four, and here was the inevitable result under a bright red subhead:

> "Can it be coincidence that brilliant Robin Rainshaw, his famous father's co-researcher, was working on stardroppers too? Up to now no one has dared to pose that question, but now it MUST BE ANSWERED!"

Oh, lord. . . .

"Mr. Cross," a mild voice said, and he glanced up. Taking the vacant place at his two-person table was a nondescript man in a cheap suit, with sandy hair and glasses and a wisp of beard on his sharp chin. Could this be a reporter who had evaded the vigilance of the staff?

Then a relay of memory clicked, and Dan recalled seeing this character among the forty or fifty in the audience at Club Cosmica last night. No good denying his identity, then. He said, "Who the hell are you?"

"My name's Norman Ferrers, Mr. Cross. We were introduced at the club last night, as you'll probably recall."

Oh, yes. This had been one of the people in the same group as Angel and Jerry, whom he'd put down as a listener rather than a talker. He said, "So what do you want?"

"Merely to talk to you, that's all. You were actually sitting next to Mr. Patrick, weren't you?"

"If you know that much, you know everything I know. And I hate being plagued by people before breakfast."

Not at all put out, Ferrers reached for one of the papers Dan had discarded. He said, turning to a center page, "This is very important, Mr. Cross. I think you should read this leader, which says what I want to say much more cogently than—"

"Waiter!" Dan said, snapping his fingers. Arriving with the promised coffee, the man looked an inquiry.

"Is this—person—a client of the hotel?"

"Not that I'm aware of, sir," the waiter murmured.

"Then what the hell is he doing bothering me? Get rid of him!'

Taking his time over setting down the coffee pot, the waiter said, "Certainly, sir." And continued to Ferrers: "The gentleman wishes to be undisturbed, and he is a guest in the hotel. I believe you're not."

There was a frozen pause; then, seeing Ferrers was not complying, he signaled to the stately maître d' on duty at the entrance, and the latter marched over. He stood about six-five, and was muscular with it, and doubtless could act as his own bouncer when required—not that this was the kind of hotel which employed bouncers. Faced with this giant, Ferrers rose, his features twisting into a nasty glare.

"I don't know whether you're a conscious traitor, Cross,

or just a fool!" he snapped. "But I promise you haven't heard the last of me!"

With pathetic dignity he allowed himself to be escorted to the door.

"What in hell did he mean by that?" Dan said under his breath, and looked at the article Ferrers had recommended as he sipped his coffee. This, he knew, was one of the more conservative of the London dailies, but carried relatively little influence.

"Not since the advent of nuclear energy has there been a new power so pregnant with possibilities and so fraught with danger as the miraculous talent which—we must now believe—is hidden in the signals from 'stardroppers.'

"Fraught with danger, because not yet brought under rational control. Pregnant with possibilities, because if such control can be obtained, the implications will be limitless...."

Who could take such cliché-ridden pontificating seriously? Dan dropped the paper on the floor and continued with the rest of them.

His spirits lightened a little as he read further. This wasn't quite the catastrophe he'd at first feared. There was a hint of jocularity in some of the news stories, and he guessed that if it hadn't been a quiet day on the international political front—at least, as quiet as one could hope for nowadays, what with umpteen brushfire wars in progress, the usual Arab-Israeli backbiting and other small change of modern times—it would never have been given such prominence. One columnist suggested that Patrick might turn up in the Bahamas suffering from loss of memory and two others hinted that someone was hoping to sell a lot of stardroppers to people needing colorable excuses to dodge the taxman.

If only I could believe that too. . . .

But he couldn't. He'd been convinced. And he was frightened.

He abandoned the breakfast he'd barely nibbled at, gathered his papers, and sneaked back up to his room. He needed to talk to someone in authority, and Redvers was the first choice.

Slamming the door behind him, he marched toward the phone, tossing the papers on the bed. He was just about to dial the Yard, when there was a click behind him, and he whirled to find Ferrers looking at him from the doorway of the bathroom.

He held a gun.

It was a somewhat elderly weapon—a P-38 Walther—but Dan drew slender consolation from that. Having assumed he was being sent on a mere fact-finding mission, his superiors in New York had suggested he bring nothing more lethal with him than a regular operative's toolkit—a neat little gadget disguised as a six-blade pocketknife, which required either the right preliminary information or a very high-powered X-ray machine to reveal its internal secrets.

There was only one logical thing to do; Dan did it. He turned, slowly, to face Ferrers, and held his hands out at his sides.

"That's better," Ferrers said with a sour chuckle, and emerged from the bathroom. He had been transformed by putting the gun in his hand, as though confidence flowed from its butt. "Now maybe we can talk properly. Sit down, keep your mouth shut, and listen to what I've got to say."

He perched on the corner of the bed and waved Dan to take the armchair near the phone.

"Did you read that article I recommended?" he went on.

"Yes," Dan said curtly. "A lot of hot air."

"You think so? Then you're either stupid or insanely optimistic. Think carefully. I know that over the past decade or so there's been a divergence of policy between your country and ours, but at bottom there remains a real identity of interest which some of us have worked to preserve. All of a sudden, it's turned out that there actually is some strange knowledge to be had from stardropper signals, and that means that those of us who care about the community of interest I mentioned have got to move *fast*. Because if somebody in the eastern bloc, and worst of all in the Maoist countries—"

By this time Dan was coming to the boil. Gun or no gun. He said, tight-lipped, "Who are you with—what group?"

"I'm a member of the Blue Front, Mr. Cross. We're the people who believe, as I imagine you do, that our anti-American policy of the past ten years or so has been calculated to deliver us into the hands of the Reds. I'm appealing to you as an American to tell us everything you can about what happened last night. We're conducting an emergency inquiry into the Patrick case, and any tiny snippet of information—"

It took Dan that long to marshal what he wanted to say, and to draw a breath deep enough to say it in one go. The Blue Front, notoriously, was one of the most reactionary groups in Europe; the Agency had tangled with it on more than one occasion. But if there was one thing which any Agency operative was required to believe, it was that a nationalist in the nuclear age was as much of an anachronism as a crusader waving his sword and yelling, "Death to the infidel!"

It was a view that Dan subscribed to without reservation.

He said, "No wonder you have to hold a gun on somebody before you can get him to listen to you! Well, it's your turn to listen to *me*! This is the twentieth century, chum! This is the age of rockets and satellites and moonships and nuclear bombs, which means it's the age when we have to give up thinking with our muscles and start using our brains! You talk about 'community of interest'—well, *my* community of interest is with the whole human race! I'm a human being first and an American second, which is the right order. *Go away!*"

For a heart-stopping instant he thought he'd overdone his counterblast to the point where Ferrers was about to shoot him down, and the hell with the consequences. But at the same instant there came a knock at the door. Overtense, like a watchspring on the point of breaking, Ferrers jerked his head around and gave Dan his chance.

Launching himself low, he hurled himself out of the chair with the full force of both arms and butted Ferrers in the chest, hurling him back on the bed. Cracking his own arm forward, he connected with Ferrer's at the elbow, and the gun went thud on the carpet. He was much heavier than Ferrers, and in addition was extremely well trained in man-to-man combat—the Agency was jealous of its operatives' ability to take care of themselves. When the bellhop, who had knocked, opened the door with a passkey, he found Dan holding Ferrers flat on his back on the bed.

"Ah—" the intruder said, and swallowed hard. "I'm sorry! When I didn't get an answer, I thought you must still be downstairs."

He offered a brown-paper package in mute justification of his entry: the Binton stardropper which Nick Carlton had brought back for him and left at the desk.

"Put that over there and come pick up this bastard's gun," Dan said, panting.

"What?" The man's eyes bulged. But he complied, and gingerly reclaimed the weapon from the floor, handing it with truly British uncertainty. It was a source of neverending wonder to Dan that in this country almost nobody had seen, let alone handled, a sidearm. As soon as the gun was in safe hands, he let Ferrers get up.

"What—happened?" the bellboy demanded.

"Oh, he was waiting for me in the bathroom," Dan sighed. "How do I reach the police in this town?"

"You just dial three nines, sir," the bellboy said. "It puts you straight through to Scotland Yard. But if you'd like us to attend to all that . . ." Gathering assurance, he turned the gun around and made as though to point it at Ferrers.

Dan deprived him of it politely. "I think I may be more used to these than you are," he murmured. "All right— call the Yard for me. But make sure you reach Superintendent Redvers. He thas a particular interest in bastards like this one."

Ferrer's face crumpled like wet paper and he sat down on the bed and started to sob.

XII

It was all attended to very discreetly; Redvers arrived in person as Dan had hoped, accompanied by two plainclothes detectives who formally arrested Ferrers on a charge of assault with a deadly weapon, to wit one Walther automatic pistol, and took him sniveling away. When he'd gone, Dan glanced at Redvers.

"You were late today," he said. "I expected you to call me up in the small hours."

"I was the one who got called up in the small hours," Redvers grunted, and rubbed his eyes. They were red-rimmed for lack of sleep. "Get me a drink on Agency funds. I need one."

"Sure." Dan went to the phone and told room service to bring up some Scotch and a bucket of ice. Sitting down, he continued, "You did know I was next to this man who went out, didn't you?"

"Next to him?" Redvers echoed. "I knew you were there, naturally, but—literally next to him?"

"In the next chair."

"Christ." Redvers gave a humorless smile. "Makes you seem like some kind of grim reaper, doesn't it? Two in one day!"

"You don't honestly think that I . . . ?" Dan let the words go before he realized. After Lilith's disappearance, and then Patrick's, the idea must have been simmering in his subconscious, ready to emerge on cue.

"No, I don't," Redvers interrupted. "But then, to be frank, I don't know what the hell to think. Any more than I did yesterday. What did that little fascist want, by the way?"

"Ferrers? Oh, he said they were conducting an inquiry

into the Patrick case, and wanted me to tell them anything I'd noticed."

"Did you notice anything?"

"I was preoccupied with the stardropper that was being demonstrated."

"You mean you were getting something out of its signals?"

"Not that I'm aware of," Dan shrugged. "But I was concentrating on it, naturally—inasmuch as one could concentrate on such a noise."

The helpful bellboy returned at that moment, bringing the promised whisky, and Dan tipped him five pounds. Looking at the money, the man said diffidently, "Mr. Cross, are you—?"

"Am I sure that's the bill I meant to give you?" Dan said gruffly. "Isn't it enough? What fee do you usually charge for saving someone's life?"

"I didn't . . ." The man swallowed hard. "Did I?"

"If you hadn't knocked when you did, I'd never have had the chance to jump the guy," Dan shrugged. "But—ah—that isn't all it's for."

"Anything else I can do for you?" the man said eagerly, folding and pocketing the money.

"Help keep those reporters out of my hair."

"Yes, *sir*!"

"He won't be able to," Redvers said as Dan handed him his drink.

"Why not?"

"You don't have the least idea what a hornet's nest has been let loose in this village. Cheers."

"I saw the morning papers—all of them."

"Most of it didn't happen until the papers were on sale," Redvers sighed. "That's how people heard, and the reaction . . . Oh Christ, it's terrifying!"

"Such as?" Dan crossed his legs and reached for a cigarette. Belated reaction to what Ferrers had done was making his hands shake and his stomach churn. But a tranquilizer would take care of that in a moment.

"You go out and see for yourself." Redvers gulped his drink and wiped his mustache with the back of his hand. "But while I think of it: is there anything you can tell me that might be helpful? Did you have any—any premonition that something big was about to happen, for instance?"

Dan thought for a while, and finally shook his head. "I can't recall anything like that," he admitted. "I was taken completely by surprise."

"And the other people present? I've seen some of them, of course, but not all by any means."

"As far as I could tell, none of them were affected any differently from me. Some of them looked physically as well as mentally shocked, and one in particular blew her stack."

"The secretary, Mrs. Towler?" And, on Dan's nod, Redvers sighed, "Yes, we had her contact us, with some wild complaint about the misconduct of the club in canceling the rest of the evening's program. . . . Ah, she's a nut, I'm afraid."

Dan hesitated. He said, "Did you talk to Angel Allen?"

"On the phone. I know her from before, of course. Why?"

"I was wondering whether I ought to go and talk to her myself. Do you have her address?"

"She's the only Angel Allen in the London phonebook," Redvers shrugged. "But you won't reach her at home right now—she works."

"Where?"

"At a mental hospital. Or rather, she works *out* of a mental hospital. She's a PSW."

"Psychiatric social worker?"

"Correct. And, since her fiancé's disappearance, she's been specializing in stardropper addicts."

"I see." Dan frowned. "Which hospital anyway?"

"St. Wenceslas."

There was a pause. Draining the last of his drink, Redvers broke it, and rose.

"Well! I don't suppose I have to tell you this is the event which has been giving me nightmares—the disappearance we can't keep quiet?"

"I learned that from the papers," Dan muttered.

"So do what I told you—go out and look the scene over for yourself. And if you draw any conclusions, I'd appreciate being the first to hear them. . . . You did file your report to the Agency, I presume?"

"Yes," Dan agreed.

"And—?"

"They'll react in their own sweet time," he snapped. "Did you look at any of the rest of today's news? We're dealing with another crisis in the Middle East, two others in black Africa, a revolution in—"

He broke off. His guard had been pierced for a moment. No outsider was supposed to comprehend the full extent of the Special Agency's operations.

But Redvers took it as a matter of course. He, at least, seemed prepared to accept the Agency at its face value.

"I guess it'll take them a day or two to figure out that this is the crisis which could trigger the big blowup," he said. "Those other things—they're routine, aren't they? I mean, we've had lots of them before and we're still on a habitable planet. But this one . . . !" He grimaced.

"One thing I have been forgetting to say," he added. "Do you need spokesmen from the Chinese, Russian, or any other embassy here? I can set that up for you whenever you like."

Accustomed to working in a country which was very definitely the opposite of neutral, Dan hadn't considered that point. He hesitated. "I'd have to clear that first," he said at length. "But I think it might be a good idea."

"Say when, and I'll lay it on." Redvers started to the door. "But don't forget, under any circumstances: whatever cooperation you need, I'll provide if it's in my power. All right?"

Departing, he left a lingering impression which greatly puzzled Dan. He seemed—as nearly as it could be defined—to be looking to Dan for something: not to the Agency, which would have been logical, but to Dan Cross personally.

Why?

Pouring himself another drink, he unwrapped the Binton 'dropper which Nick Carlton had brought back for him. He checked it over. It was exactly as he had last seen it, down to the knot in the sling which Lilith had slashed. For a few minutes he listened to it absently, as though he could retrieve the answers to all his questions from the random noises it emitted.

Abruptly he cut the power, shut the case, and emptied his glass. It was useless making guesses, more useless still sitting here with the earpiece in and concentrating on weird—alien?—sounds. He needed to do what Redvers had suggested, look the scene over for himself and draw what conclusions he could.

And Cosmica Limited, in easy walking distance, would be an excellent place to start.

Cosmica Limited was full. People were struggling and jostling one another not only inside but on the street in front of the store, and two policemen were trying to prevent them interfering with the passage of cars. Occasionally they had to force a way for someone trying to leave. As Dan approached, he saw them perform this service for a middle-aged man with a shiny new white-cased instrument —a Gale and Welchman of the type Watson had demonstrated (and also the type Lilith had been hooked by, he reminded himself). Hurrying away, the man was trailed by a half a dozen other people offering to pay inflated prices for the instrument rather than wait their turn in the long line outside the store.

Redver's gloomy prophecy was being fulfilled.

One couldn't yet call the situation hysterical. It was no worse than what could be seen at the bargain sales of a big department store. But already there was a fearful greed in the eyes of the purchasers who were emerging from the shop, an obsessional tightness about the hands which clutched their new possessions. It made Dan's scalp crawl.

He was well above average height, and as part of his Agency training he had been taught to exploit this fact when necessary. He bore himself commandingly into the midst of the crowd, and people gave way without quite realizing why, even apologizing when he pushed in front of them. He contrived to enter the store ahead of at least twenty who had arrived earlier.

Once inside, progress became more difficult, but he had the advantage that he was not interested in buying one of the stardroppers on display, only in working his way to the main sales counter at the back, whereas everyone else had at least half an eye on the rapidly diminishing range of instruments available. Three or four of the dozen-odd shelves had already been stripped bare.

The staff—supplemented by four young men who didn't

look like sales clerks, but more like warehousemen—were growing harassed and irritable. Arriving within a few places of the counter, Dan caught the eye of the pretty brown girl who had served him before, as she shook back hair from her face. Recognizing him, she rolled her eyes skyward as if to say, "This is a madhouse!" And was at once called back to her job, even though a moment earlier she had sold another instrument to a client so eager to try his purchase out that he hadn't waited for her to make change before turning and struggling back toward the exit.

Directly between Dan and the counter were two men in business suits, one of them carrying what Dan took at first glance to be a stardropper. It wasn't. It was a press camera, and—as became clear when the brown girl came to attend to his companion—the pair were journalists who hadn't yet given up hope of finding some new slant on the big story of the day.

He didn't catch what the photographer's companion said, but he heard the girl's answer because it was shrill with impatience. Probably she'd answered the same question fifty times already this morning.

"No, Mr. Watson *isn't* available, I don't know where he is, and I don't know when he'll be back!"

The reporter persisted. Obviously bored, the cameraman nudged him.

"Jack, why don't you just put it down that he vanished up his stardropper too?" he suggested cynically.

Jack gave him a scowl. Other customers clamored for the girl's attention, and she made to move on. But the reporter tapped her arm, delaying her.

"Miss! Uh—while I'm here, I think I'll take the chance and buy one of your stardroppers!"

The girl slammed the firm's catalog down before him. She said in a hard voice, "Numbers five through nine, twenty-nine, and forty-two are out of stock. We have all the others. I'll be back when you've made up your mind.

"Jack, you're not falling for this too?" said the cameraman.

"I don't know," Jack said slowly, turning the pages. "I don't know."

It took Dan nearly ten minutes to get out of the store again, and the crush around the entrance was worse than ever. Seeing he had bought nothing—he had left his own instrument at the hotel—a sly-faced man hanging around the fringe of the crowd sidled up to him.

"Say, I have good bargains in stardroppers if you want one. I have good, scarcely used instruments of the highest quality. Prices ridiculously low, you understand." He winked. "Not so many in stock but I can always get you whatever you want in two-three days for slight extra charge. Give you examples. Hand-made American 'droppers for fifty pounds in cash. Regular British instruments for twenty-five and up—"

Dan ignored him. The chances were excellent he was offering stolen goods. That was another inescapable consequence of the impact of the news about Leon Patrick. Overnight a profitable black market would have been created in the instruments.

"Well, you might at least have said a polite thank you!" the sly-faced man said huffily to Dan's retreating back, and turned to accost another, more tractable prospect.

On most other people's faces there was a look of eager excitement. Dan, by contrast, felt his own features fold into a scowl. Suddenly there was an unhealthy odor in the air: the smell of frenzy.

It made him want to call up his headquarters on a clear line and file another report, in plain language this time, underlining everything he'd said yesterday about the dangers inherent in the situation here. But there seemed to be no point. The Agency maintained around-the-clock news-monitoring service; they'd have heard about Patrick's disappearance the moment it went out on the satellite beams, and they'd have noted, without doubt, that he'd already foreshadowed such an occurrence in his report of a few hours earlier.

Which would have enchanced his reputation as one of the Agency's outstanding operatives. But right now that felt like small comfort. All too probably, when *this* crisis reached critical mass, there wouldn't be an Agency to pick up the pieces. . . .

Time hadn't yet run out, though. And until it finally did it was his job to keep the data flowing in. The press had tracked down Angel, Jerry, and Watson; he ought, he decided, to do at least as much. Watson, he could assume, was out of reach—he'd heard as much from the girl in the store, and had no reason to doubt what she'd said to the reporter. If he'd been in Watson's position, he'd have gone into hiding.

It might be worth checking with Angel, though. Not simply because she'd been engaged to Robin Rainshaw, but—far more importantly—because she, like Jerry, was a long-time stardropper fan, and being much better educated and more articulate than Lilith might be able to clarify things that he still found confusing.

He made for the first phone booth he spotted, and was on the point of dialing the number he found against her name—as Redvers had said, she was the only Angel Allen in the book—when he checked and turned instead to the number of the St. Wenceslas Hospital. There was a separate line listed for the PSW department, under "Outpatients and Aftercare." He rang it.

To the voice that answered he said, "Miss Angel Allen, please."

"Not another bloody reporter?" the voice snapped. "Because if so—"

"No, I'm not a reporter. It's Dan Cross calling."

"Just a second." Muffled in the background, an exchange of question and answer, and then Angel herself came to the phone.

"Morning, Dan," she said dispiritedly. "What is it?"

"I was wondering if I might drop by and talk to you," Dan said.

"I'd rather you didn't. This has been a hell of a morning. I ought to be out on my rounds, but when I tried to leave my office I was bloody pounced on by a crowd of—oh, I don't know what to call them except *madmen*! Ex-patients, some of the people I've had in care in the past, practically all the current ones . . . We actually had to call the police to keep guard and stop them breaking into the building. It's like a riot!"

"Are they after you personally?"

"Of course. It's the—the magical contagion bit, I suppose. They think I'd be a sort of lucky charm for their own success."

That figured. Dan glanced across the street toward Cosmica Limited. A bus had just pulled up, and a group of six or eight eager people had jumped off it, heading for the store entrance. On seeing the milling throng that blocked their way, they had stopped dead in simultaneous dismay.

"But"—Angel was continuing—"if you want to talk to someone about what happened last night, you should get on to Jerry Bartlett. He called me earlier and asked if I knew where you could be reached."

"Fine. What's his number?"

"Oh, you'll find his firm in the directory. He works for Tarquin Telecommunications, at their research division in Chiswick."

"Thanks very much. By the way, I don't suppose you know how I can get hold of Walter Watson, do you?"

"No. If he's neither in the store nor at home. Is he hiding out, then?"

"I imagine so."

"Lucky devil," she said with a trace of bitterness. "Wish I could. My phone was ringing all night from midnight on, and I lost half my sleep. And now, after what's been happening here, I don't know why in hell I bothered to come to the office today. I'm never going to get any work done in these conditions."

She cut the connection with a snort of annoyance. There was a knock on the door of Dan's phone booth, and he saw a face glowering through the glass. He scowled back and took out the directory S to Z, looking for Jerry's firm.

He reached the physicist at once, and was promptly invited to come straight out to the lab.

"Thanks very much," he said, and went to find a taxi.

XIII

The Tarquin Telecommunications research and development center was in a large 1930's building partly overshadowed by a dual-level expressway. Weathered into its frontage, only half-concealed by a big new illuminated sign, were the outlines of letters which identified the place as having formerly belonged to a perfume manufacturer.

As well as a company watchman on duty at the main gate, there was also a harried-looking police constable. Dan was made to wait in his cab while the watchman called Jerry's office and confirmed that he was here by invitation.

"Sorry about that, sir," the man said when he'd done so. "But we've been plagued all morning by a gang of nuts. We only just managed to freeze them off." He nodded at the constable. "Had to run three of them in because they threatened to start smashing the windows."

"What was it all about?" Dan said, feigning ignorance.

"Oh, this stardropper nonsense." The watchman was about fifty, and his tone was of elderly cynicism. "What it's got to make them so worked up, *I* don't know. Who'd want to vanish into thin air and never come back? I mean, if you're that sick of life, there are lots of other ways of bowing out, aren't there? Quietly, so you don't cause anyone else any trouble!"

Shaking his head, he waved Dan's cab on to the main entrance.

He was paying the driver off when he heard his name called, and turned to find Jerry Bartlett hurrying down the steps from the wide glass front doors. He looked even more harassed than he had yesterday evening.

"Glad you could stop by!" he exclaimed. "I've been desperately trying to reach Wally Watson, but he's nowhere to be found, and Angel has this trouble at the hospital with all these idiots who seem to think she can help them do what Leon did—if he *did* do anything, and didn't have it simply happen to him. . . . Well, come on up to the lab and let's see if we can thrash anything out, hm?"

"Such as what?" Dan, though he had far longer legs, was having difficulty keeping up with the pace Jerry was setting down the long corridors of the building.

"Christ, how should I know?" Jerry ran his fingers through his hair. "Whatever happened, however it happened, it doesn't fit the orthodox laws of science. But you've at least met Berghaus, haven't you? He may have mentioned something to you which he hasn't published yet, for example. Up these stairs—just the one flight." He pointed to the left.

"Why haven't you tried to reach Berghaus himself, then?" Dan demanded.

"Think I haven't? But everybody's after him! I put a call through directly I got home last night—traced him in the *Who's Who of Physics*—but he wasn't in, and when I tried again an hour later I found he'd told his local exchange to block all incoming calls."

"Well, how about Rainshaw?" Dan suggested as they reached the top of the stairs and Jerry marched ahead to fling open a door opposite.

"Rainshaw has an unlisted number, and has had ever since his son disappeared. I don't suppose you know him, do you?"

"I've met him," Dan admitted.

"Do you know where he lives?"

"I'm afraid not. I was taken to see him at his lab."

"Blast! He's at the DAPR place at Richmond, and you aren't allowed to reach him at work without a Home Office authorization."

"Dapper?" Dan echoed, puzzled.

"Department of Advanced Physical Research," Jerry clarified. Swinging around the corner of a large desk cluttered with miscellaneous electronic parts, he dropped into a chair and waved Dan to take another facing him. "Well! Coffee? Beer? Cigarette? I don't smoke, but I have some here for visitors." He opened a box and pushed it in Dan's direction.

Dan took one with a mutter of thanks and looked around the office. One wall was entirely of glass to below waist-height, its sill heaped with papers and files. Another was a single large Formica sheet on which a critical-path analysis of what seemed to be a very complex experimental program had been inscribed with a china-marking pencil. Next to the door were shelves on aluminum supports, containing about five or six stardroppers and boxes of spare parts for them, and behind Jerry's desk were a case of reference books and two information-retrieval computer keyboards sited where he could reach them without leaving his chair.

Clearing a bulky file from the top of his desk intercom, he ordered coffee to be brought, and leaned back with a deep breath.

"I suppose I didn't dream it, did I?" he said to Dan.

"I've been wishing the same thing," Dan admitted. "Have you heard what's happening at Cosmica this morning?"

"No, but I can imagine. There's a little shop I pass on my way from home to the station every day, which sells stardroppers as well as radios and records, and at eight-thirty today there were at least a dozen people lined up outside waiting for it to open at nine."

"You have the picture, then. And you saw the papers?"

"Naturally. It'll be interesting to hear what the radio news says at one o'clock; they have an in-depth program then, instead of these two-minute snippets."

"Interesting!" Dan gave a humorless smile.

"Yes." Jerry stared out of the window at the upper level of the expressway; the lab was efficiently sound-proofed, and the traffic was roaring past in silence. "You know, that was all it was for me, to begin with. We got into this field—my firm, I mean—along with just about every other telecommunications company on the planet, purely because we wanted to know if this 'Rainshaw effect' might lead to some new kind of information-transmitting technique. I mean, the radio bands are so overcrowded nowadays, at least in the advanced countries. So one morning I was whistled into old Tinker's office—the director of research—and asked if I'd like my own department and a fifty-thousand-pound initial budget to investigate these things, and obviously I said yes please, when can I start?

So they gave me a couple of technicians and a secretary, and I built half a dozen of the damned things in a week—not realizing, to be honest, they were protected by a patent application. And of course that was before this horrible name 'stardropper' got hung on them. There are a couple of my originals behind you, on the shelf: the ones screwed to wooden baseboards." He pointed, and Dan glanced at the instruments, laid out in extended order in typical breadboard style.

"And I'd been happily fiddling around with them for a month or more, measuring signal strengths, trying to correlate patterns from different instruments, and so on, when all of a sudden I woke up one morning and realized I didn't have the *foggiest* idea what was going on. I mean, I was like a kid in front of a big computer pushing buttons to see the pretty red and green lights flash! Which was what convinced me that looking for a new communications mode in stardroppers was futile. We were confronted by a totally new phenomenon, unforeseen, inexplicable. So I went back to Tinker and I told him straight out: you're going to have to face the fact that this isn't going to produce commercial results of the kind you're after, but for all we can tell right now it may overturn the whole of traditional physics, so can I have twice the budget and an extra six assistants? And—bless him—he gave me the money and four more people. And then of course Berghaus published his theory, and I'd proved my point. But nothing else except that. Honestly, we're no further forward than we were the day his theory appeared!"

Dan tapped his ash into a wastebasket. He said, "But I'd have thought—"

"We'd have established a few facts? Oh, sure! All negative. Whatever the signals may derive from, they incontestably do not travel by any conventional route. They are almost beyond doubt not subject to the inverse-square law. They may be truly instantaneous, though so far we haven't figured out how to measure a speed greater than light's. I wish someone would find the tachyon and give us information from the other side of the C-barrier! But didn't Berghaus tell you about this kind of thing?"

"I didn't ask about this aspect of it much when I met him. I'm not a trained physicist, you see. I was more concerned with the results of people becoming convinced that the signals contain alien knowledge."

Jerry nodded. "Shame! I'm sure that man *must* have new insights by now, which he hasn't published yet. . . . But our main problem, you know, is simply not knowing where to begin! For instance, I came up with a hypothesis that the signals may possibly use local gravitational fields as—well, as a sort of resonator, even though it's minuscule, and the likeliest source in my view is the potential energy of the stressed-space area surrounding this ball of rock, or maybe the entire solar system. Follow me?"

"Not really," Dan confessed.

"Hmm! What can I compare it to? Oh, yes! Think of a piano. Or perhaps better would be a spring, under tension because a weight is hanging from it. You hit the right frequency on a tuning fork, and you'll get sympathetic vibrations from the spring. Take the weight away, so the spring goes slack, and it won't react to the frequency you used before—probably won't react detectably to any outside noise until you reach the point where the blast effect takes over."

"So how would you go about checking that?" Dan asked.

"Obviously, fly a 'dropper aboard a satellite," Jerry shrugged. "So I've put in applications to everywhere I can think of where they're launching spacecraft—Kennedy, Woomera, Baikonur . . . I *think* I may have struck lucky with the Swedes at Kiruna; they wrote me the other day to say that if I can cut the mass of the experiment down below a hundred and sixty grams, I can have space in their next meteorological satellite. But I'm waiting now to find out what other instruments they're flying, because I'll need to know how much shielding from local interference I have to build into the 'dropper. I'm afraid it may be too much to meet the weight limit."

"And if you turn out to be right in your suspicion?"

Jerry gave a harsh chuckle. "One more on the list of negative facts! Yesterday I was overjoyed with my chance to get a 'dropper into space. Today I have this feeling Wally Watson was right all along, and I'm wasting my time digging into the microcosmic aspects when there are macro effects under my bloody nose!"

"Watson puzzles me," Dan said slowly. "How did you first come to know him?"

"Oh, just by enrolling in Club Cosmica. You see, after they gave me my nice fat budget and my new staff, I ran out of ideas, and it really started to get under my hide, I can tell you. I mean, imagine me with all that money and these labs and five assistants, and sitting around chewing my nails! So—"

He was interrupted by a knock on the door, and without waiting for an answer a pretty girl came in carrying two cups of coffee. "Ah!" he said. "Thanks, Shirley. This is my secretary, by the way—Shirley Brown, Dan Cross."

They exchanged nods.

"How are things outside?" Jerry asked.

"Oh!" She pulled a face. "I'm still spending half my time telling callers you're not here, of course. Goodness knows how many there've been so far today, but I imagine over fifty. And as soon as you're free, by the way, Charlie Potts wants you to come and see the signal he's getting from that new 'dropper of his. He's split it three ways and fed it to a color TV screen, and it's making beautiful patterns."

"Okay, I will," Jerry sighed. "Meantime, don't let him just sit in front of it, will you? He's a dangerously good hypnotic subject, and he might go into a trance!"

"I'll tell him," Shirley said. And added, on the point of turning away, "Incidentally, Jerry—!"

"Yes?"

"I've—uh—I've decided I'd like to buy a stardropper. What would you recommend me to get, that isn't too expensive?"

"Oh Christ," Jerry said. "You too? Well, it's supposed to be a free country. . . . Dan, what do you think? You have that very advanced Binton, I think Wally said."

"Well, what he advised me to try was a Gale and Welchman," Dan said. "And I must admit it's about the only instrument I've run across which really impressed me."

"Gale and Welchman," Shirley repeated thoughtfully. "Thanks—I'll try and pick one up."

She went out.

"Where were we?" Jerry said, stirring sugar into his cup.

"I was asking how you met Wally Watson," Dan said.

"Oh yes. Well, I was getting desperate for new angles to try, so I saw an ad for this new club—I think they'd just had their first or second meeting—and I enrolled, and as I'd hoped I found a whole bunch of people there who were in the same state as I was: baffled and infuriated and eager to swap suggestions. Matter of fact, you said you met Dr. Rainshaw, didn't you?"

"Yes. Is he a member of Club Cosmica?"

"Oh no! But about the second person I met after Wally was Robin Rainshaw, his son. Angel's fiancé, you know."

Dan gave a thoughtful nod. "Did you know him well?"

"Not very. Casually and professionally. And then, of course, he—uh—disappeared. Angel was absolutely broken up by it. Who wouldn't have been?"

"Did you believe at first that he'd really disappeared, like Leon Patrick?"

"Hell, of course I didn't! I don't even want to believe Leon disappeared!" Jerry gulped at his coffee, burned his tongue, and swore, grabbing for a pack of tissues.

"Have you any idea at *all* how it might have happened?"

"None. I went back with Jock to his hotel when the pub shut last night, and we sat in the bar there for an hour arguing, but the poor guy was dead beat because he'd come down on an overnight train and he hadn't had much sleep, so I had to leave him in the end. And then I sat up myself half the night, cudgeling my brains, and answering phone calls from the papers and TV news service. . . . And I'm none the wiser. I really do think Wally's been right all along." He sounded depressed at making the admission.

"Talking about—what was your term?—the macro effects?"

"Exactly. His attitude has always been that—hmm! What was that nice analogy he once used? A biological one." Jerry frowned briefly. "Ah, I have it. He said what I was doing was like the man who proved that grasshoppers hear with their legs because when he amputated the legs they didn't jump in response to a sudden noise. I was a bit narked when he told me that, frankly, but the more I think about it, the more I feel he may have been right."

Dan chuckled. He made a mental note to track down

Watson, however long it took. Everything he had so far been told by members of the club, added to what he himself had figured out while talking to Watson, indicated that this man was indeed far more than a mere store manager.

"Would you say Watson has a lot of influence on the stardropping movement?" he asked.

"Nobody I know has more," Jerry declared. "Apart from running the store, he edits the club's bulletin, and that's the most authoritative publication in the field in Britain, much more influential than any of the commercial magazines. It's the nearest approach to a proper scientific journal in the field; most of the published papers apart from that have been in regular physical journals, not specialist ones."

"Is he a scientist himself?"

"Funnily enough, yes. He mentioned it once. He trained as a neurophysiologist, and gave it up."

"To manage Cosmica Limited?"

"Manage? He owns the whole bloody show—owns the building, lives in the penthouse. But I don't know whether he genuinely set out to become a crusader, or whether he just saw there was going to be a terrific boom in stardroppers and talked other people into investing in his idea. Not that it makes much difference. You're new to this game, aren't you?"

"Yes."

"Well, it's habit-forming. Believe me. I've been eating, breathing, and sleeping stardroppers for months—not because I'm hooked, the way some of these poor bastards are that you see wandering around in a permanent daze or having hysterics on the street, but simply because knowing something is going on in the universe which the theories I was brought up to believe in don't account for gives me a kind of itch inside my skull, and I have to—to keep scratching it. Follow me?"

"I'm getting to the same state," Dan acknowledged with a sigh.

"We all do. And I think that may have happened to Wally. However he got into the game in the first place, there's no doubt he's utterly convinced of the importance of what he's doing. What's more, he conveys a sense of confidence to other people. I'm not sure I really like him, because sometimes he's offhand—almost contemptuous—about my work. But if I get discouraged, if I start to think I'm being a fool spending so much time on this subject, he's the guy I'd go to, to get talked out of my fit of the blues."

There was a pause, during which Dan finished his coffee. Suddenly Jerry slapped his desk and rose.

"Well, since you're here, you might care to look over the labs. Not that this is a typical day, I'm afraid. So far just about *no* work has been done. The first hour after I got here I spent assuring everybody that yes, as far as I can tell someone did physically vanish from Club Cosmica, and no, I haven't the least idea how it happened. Which has kind of spread a pall of gloom around the premises. But come on anyway. You can at least see Charlie's pretty three-color patterns."

XIV

At any other time the tour of the laboratory might have been fascinating. The colored display on the TV screen was indeed pretty, reminding Dan of some of the computer-programmed cosmoramic projections he'd seen, just coming into fashion in the States thanks to the availability at long last of TV tubes no deeper than a picture frame. And certainly everyone on Jerry's team seemed to have a deep personal involvement with his work; they barely interrupted their heated discussions to acknowledge his presence.

But Jerry had said in almost so many words that they didn't really know where their research was taking them, and in view of what he knew to be going on all over London, and perhaps by now all over the world, he found himself growing more and more impatient.

There had been that passing reference to Charlie Potts as a good hypnotic subject; the words had taken root in his subconscious and were sprouting ideas. They did not in fact come across him in trance before his color screen—he was too busy making adjustments to the conventional electronic equipment connecting the TV to the stardropper, changing the relationship betwen the incoming signal and the projected image and recording the effects. But . . .

Well, it was notorious that in certain abnormal mental states, including a hypnotic trance, the human being was capable of improbable feats: displays of incredible strength, for example, or recollection of the minutest details of some otherwise long-forgotten past event. Could stardropping induce some form of trance, then, in which data were put together by the mind which ordinarily the rational faculties would dismiss as ridiculous?

It was worth making inquiries about. And, of all the

sources of information he had access to, the best would be the Agency's own headquarters in New York. Long experience with ultra-advanced mental techniques such as the personal codes provided for its operatives implied that there if anywhere he could get an immediate and authoritative verdict on his guess.

Accordingly he took his leave of Jerry, with many thanks, and returned to the center of London. The Agency had an office here, as in all the major capitals of the world, and even though according to Redvers its staff had stoutly denied knowledge of his existence, it was the best place to put in a plain-language call from to his headquarters. Whether or not his hotel room was bugged, he didn't want to have to wait for a connection over regular commercial circuits.

On his way—not directly to the office, but to an intersection within easy walking distance—he realized it was as well he'd left his stardropper at the hotel. All along the sidewalks he saw people carrying 'droppers being accosted by total strangers, some blatantly and some shyly inquiring whether they were willing to part with them. He saw a placard for an evening paper which headlined a rocketing rise in the shares of stardropper manufacturers, and another which announced the theft of a truck loaded with twenty thousand pounds' worth of the instruments.

Checking his watch, he found that it was just on one o'clock, and asked the driver of his cab to switch on the radio news. The calm voice of the BBC announcer purred from a speaker in the roof of the vehicle.

"—but there was no comment from Professor Viktor Berghaus at his Long Island home. Elsewhere expert opinion appears to be divided, some authorities regarding the whole affair as a hoax, others stating that the Berghaus hypothesis implies the possibility of such events although they are unwilling to commit themselves without further study of the matter. Later in the program we shall be hearing interviews with a number of leading scientists. Meantime, there is no doubt about the general public's unqualified acceptance of the story. Most shops selling stardroppers sold out their entire stock this morning, and in some cases queues are reported to have stretched for hundreds of yards. On the London Stock Exchange the shares of all stardropper manufacturers at least doubled in price, and one of the leading international producers—"

"Here you are, guv!" the driver called.

Dan roused himself and got out. By the sound of it, he wasn't likely to learn more from the radio news than what he'd already deduced: Redvers's gloomy prophecy was being borne out.

Waiting for the cab to lose itself in the stream of traffic, he reviewed what he was going to say to New York, and then headed down the sidestreet in which the local office of the Agency was located.

The duty officer was not pleased to see him. Checking his credentials, he said, "Weren't you supposed to be here on a Grade E mission?"

"Yes."

"So why have you come openly to—?"

"I've upgraded the mission," Dan snapped. "Dammit, man, haven't you seen what's happening? This country's going collectively out of its skull! The so-called 'experts' are running in little circles—I've spent the morning talking to one of them—and just about everyone else is completely convinced a stardropper gives you the power to work miracles!" He consciously echoed Redvers's phrase. "Can you think of a more sensitive area for such a thing to happen, except maybe Israel? Come on, get me to a phone and give me a direct line to New York."

The man handed the credentials back. He said defensively, "Well, I was only—"

"Sticking to the book," Dan cut in. "This isn't *in* the book. It's incredible, impossible, and unscientific, but it's happening!"

Fortunately, although it was still barely breakfasttime in New York, one of the Agency's top psychologists was in his office. Dan had rather hoped for the man who had prepared his own personal code, but this was a better break than he had any right to expect.

"Milton Gauss here," the man said. "You landed in the middle of a hornet's nest, didn't you? I've spent the past hour using your report as a lever to budge people from their cozy beds, but so far I haven't managed to get anything constructive done. These news stories—they're true?"

"Yes."

"Any ideas?"

Dan ran briefly over his day's experiences, stressing the prompt reaction of the Blue Front, and Gauss whistled.

"They're a nasty bunch, aren't they? Have you checked out the various Maoist countries' reaction yet?"

"I intend to. Superintendent Redvers promised me contacts at any embassy I asked for."

"They'll have plenty in the London office," Gauss said. "Use those up first. Go on."

Dan continued, ending with his guess about hypnosis, and could almost hear Gauss's frown when he answered.

"I think some work's been done on that," he said. "Can't remember who did it, but I can punch for the reference. And, speaking of punching: I was just having your yesterday's report computed for trends, so I might as well add in what you've just been saying. It's on tape, of course. Hang on while I make up a keyword list for it."

There was a pause. Faintly, Dan could hear clicking noises. What Gauss was doing was feeding a recognition program into one of the Agency's computers, instructing it to sift the material of his report and propose the optimum series of further steps.

"There," the psychologist said at length. "That'll only take a moment. Now I'll get you that reference I mentioned; you can probably track down the journal in one of the big London libraries. Ah—'hypnosis'—'stardropper/ing'—and I guess we'd better have 'Rainshaw effect' too. . . ."

Click-click.

"Yes, here we are. *The Cosmica Papers*, No. 12—"

"What?" Dan jerked in his chair.

"*Cosmica Papers*, No. 12," Gauss repeated. "Are you getting this? 'Reactions of Hypnotized Subjects to the Emanations of Stardroppers,' by Walter K. Watson, B.Sc., Dipl. Neur. Oh!" Gauss checked. "The same Watson who runs that store over there?"

"Looks like it, doesn't it?" Dan muttered.

"Hmm! Interesting! And what's more, here comes your printout of immediate next steps, and guess what heads the list?"

"Find Watson."

"Precisely. Think you can?"

"I'll do my best. Are you going to send me some reinforcements?"

"Yes. Want me to put the local operatives under your direction?"

Dan hesitated. "I'm not sure I'd tell them to do more than I imagine they're doing already," he said.

"Well, I'll make double-sure they *are* doing it," Gauss said. "I'll telex a memo to London rating this stardropper thing an A-1 Red priority. You've seen what the Chinese and Russians have been saying, have you?"

"I only caught a snatch of the radio news at one. I imagine the noon papers will be carrying it, though. But tell me the gist."

"Oh, mainly that this is a filthy plot to undermine the confidence of their people in the leadership. The whole story is rumor, rubbish, garbage—" Gauss snorted. "But they're alarmed, to put it mildly. They've never been able to make sense of the British since they went neutralist, any more than the American government can. What do you make of the country, by the way? It's your first visit, isn't it?"

"Yes. And *I* don't know what the hell to make of it, either. It could be a giant madhouse, or it could be full of people who are so far ahead of the rest of us we can't keep up."

"Speaking of madhouses, we've got one in California, apparently. The National Guard is out in Berkeley again— first time in five years. And things look bleak in India and Japan, too. There's rioting."

"Oh, Christ," Dan sighed wearily. "Sometimes I wonder if it's worth it. . . . Well, never mind. I'll go chase Watson."

"Just pray he hasn't disappeared down his stardropper too," Gauss said caustically, and broke the connection.

On his way back from the Agency office to Oxford Street and Cosmica Limited, Dan bought the evening papers and found that Gauss hadn't been exaggerating. For some reason this scrap of news had triggered off a worldwide reaction, and it wasn't confined to the countries where stardropping was a popular private pastime, either.

Reading between the lines of the statements issued from Peking—where stardropping was considered "antisocial" —and Moscow—where it was considered "antiscientific"— one could see that an incredibly violent response must have been generated, as though this was exactly what everyone had been waiting for without realizing. There was reference to people filching the necessary electronics parts to make 'droppers from state-owned factories; these "enemies of the people, robbing their brothers," were promised the full rigor of the law. Absentees from work were also threatened, and that meant that literally thousands—conceivably, millions—must have stayed away from their jobs. Ordinarily, the Eastern countries, both Leninist and Maoist, kept labor problems very quiet.

And in Hong Kong and Osaka, the two big Oriental centers of stardropper manufacture, employees were reported to be switching on the completed instruments and listening to them with mad desperate hunger, while empty trucks waited at the gates to take away the day's output. And in Paris . . .

Dan rolled the papers together and shoved them into a litter basket. How long before the governments of the great powers realized that the rumors were finally confirmed as truth, and *someone else had the secret first?*

Because when that moment came . . .

XV

Outside Cosmica Limited the crush was worse than ever, and police had had to be called to control the line of eager would-be purchasers. The recent arrivals appeared to be office-workers who had decided to sacrifice their lunch hours; by the look of things, they wouldn't be back to work on time.

From the opposite side of the roadway Dan surveyed the building. It was almost brand-new. The whole of this area had been redeveloped as part of the government's massive program to absorb the manpower and materials liberated by their disarmament policy. To eliminate congestion caused by delivery trucks unloading, most such modern blocks, he knew, were designed around an access road or tunnel parallel to the street. So where was the nearest entrance to the back of Cosmica?

He found it about a quarter-mile along the street, where a sloping ramp dived sharply under a small public arcade, with benches, a fountain, and flowering shrubs in stone pots. There was a railed-off pedestrian way; he marched smartly down it.

Spotting the rear entrance to Cosmica posed no problem, either. Backed up to one of the delivery bays was a large truck lettered with the name GALE AND WELCHMAN, BIRMINGHAM, and several eager would-be stardropper owners were clustered around it, trying to bribe the men unloading its cargo to sell them instruments straight from the packing cases.

Dan took advantage of the distraction they were causing to make his way unchallenged to the door through which the cases were being taken. Shortly, a harassed apprentice in brown overalls came toward him pushing a huge cardboard carton on a hand trolley. With all the aplomb he could muster Dan held the door open for him, and the boy noticed him only long enough to mutter thanks. He did not question Dan's right to follow him inside.

There, Dan found himself facing more doors, swinging shut, which presumably gave onto Cosmica Limited's stockrooms. To his right, however, there was a narrow corridor. He followed it, turned a sharp corner, and discovered a flight of dusty stairs—logically, a fire exit. Without hesitation he started up them. It was a long climb, and at every bend of the stairs he half expected to meet a reporter, or a member of the Blue Front, or someone else who had located Watson's home address and was equally eager to get hold of him.

Of course, maybe that had already happened during the morning, and by now everyone else was satisfied that Watson was not in fact in his apartment.

Dan didn't care whether he was or not. A vacant home could often be nearly as informative as its occupier.

At the very top of the stairs, he found himself on a luxuriously carpeted landing. There was hardly a sound. Efficient insulation plus the effect of height muted even the busy roar of Oxford Street. There was an elevator door, closed. There was a frosted-glass window, alongside which a red-handled hammer hung in a glass-fronted case; a notice said that if the internal stairs were blocked by fire, the hammer should be used to smash the window and gain access to an outside escape. Glancing back, he realized he had left footprints in a faint layer of dust on the staircase by which he had climbed up.

Dead opposite the elevator shaft was the only other door. It bore neither a number nor a name, but there was a buzzer in the middle of it.

He thumbed it, heard it faintly inside the apartment, and waited. Nothing happened. While waiting an extra couple of minutes for safety's sake, he inspected the edge of the doorframe. Tiny metal tabs were visible between the door and the jamb. He identified them as the terminals of one of the commonest European alarm systems, an Italian brand called Protex. In which case he could get inside with only a little trouble.

He took out his pocket knife, gave it the twist and slide which opened its hidden interior compartments, and selected a number of very fine wires, which he used to link the alarm tabs. Then he applied multiple picklocks to the various locks on the door—there were three—and gently, gently eased it open. He raised the carpet just inside the door to make certain he wasn't about to step on a pressure-sensitive pad—there wasn't one—and went in.

The apartment was small, but furnished and decorated. Leaving the door ajar, he walked rapidly around it once to confirm that in fact the place was unoccupied. All clear. Shutting the door, he began a more intensive inspection. First, he needed an emergency escape route, and that was simple enough to find: Watson's bedroom had an openable window from which it was possible to reach the fire escape.

Feeling no need to hurry, because Watson was almost certainly planning to stay away for some while to elude the press, he worked his way around the lounge, paying special attention to an unlocked bureau in which he found a great many papers, books, and notebooks. Some of them referred to stardropping, but as far as a cursory inspection revealed they were connected with Watson's job or with the Club Cosmica, which was only to be expected. It wasn't until he had gone out to the bedroom that he ran across anything peculiar.

What in hell was the man doing with a diving suit hung up in his wardrobe?

Dan stared in disbelief. Yes, a diving suit. He recognized it as one of Siebe and Gorman's modern ultralight-weight outfits, made of scarlet imperviflex for easy seeing under water. It looked almost new. On a shelf above it he found the goldfish-bowl helmet, a quarter the weight of a conventional metal one, and also a sealed camera, and propped in the back corner of the closet a set of oxygen tanks. According to the meters, they were full and ready for use.

Who in the world would make a hobby out of suit-diving nowadays? Who had ever done so?

He looked again, some incongruity itching at the back of his mind, and realized: no boots. For suit-diving boots with weighted soles were essential. There were none here, nor in any of the other closets.

What he did find during his further search, however,

was a small portable file unit, the type designed to be carried like a dispatch case. It was locked, but the catch yielded to a few seconds' work with his pocket knife. Inside he found a great many typed notes, mostly headed "CPF" and bearing various dates from a year ago to about two months ago. Most of them were lists of numbers with brief notes in a comments column at the right, such as "Unconfirmed" and "This one definite!!!"

What was unconfirmed or definite, there was nothing to explain. Abandoning that problem for the moment, he investigated the last closet. Here he found a box of color slides, the right size to fit the sealed camera he had already seen. But these were not underwater scenes. Where the landscapes might be which they showed, he could only guess; he hazarded they were from places he hadn't visited, in Australia or South America, for they showed thick dark greenery and red-yellow desert with eroded rock formations. Without a magnifying glass or a proper projector, their scale was too small for him to make out the fine detail, so after glancing through a score or so he put them back.

And the only other peculiar thing in the closet was a sack of rocks, which equally told him nothing since he knew little about mineralogy.

Replacing them precisely as they had been, he went to take another look at the file of notes, the only promising thing he'd so far chanced across. This time he found a handwritten sheet he had previously disregarded, and on it found what the abbreviation "CPF" stood for. The writer—Watson, presumably—had put:

"Straightforward enough. It's the cocktail-party factor, and there's no avoiding that."

Dan frowned. That was a standard slang term in information theory, the nickname for the process of sorting a particular series of data from a jumble of background noise, like carrying on a conversation with one other person in competition with fifty more talking at the top of their lungs. It might, obviously, be relevant to stardropper investigations, but what the actual relevance might be . . .

A point suddenly struck him. Putting the notes away as neatly as he could, he made another round of the apartment, looking for a stardropper. There wasn't a single one in the place, and that seemed strange. Granted, Watson could have his pick of the stock held by the firm downstairs, but even so the typical pattern seemed to be that each user of a stardropper became attached to some particular instrument. Nick Carlton, for example, owned six jointly with his wife. Was Watson so fond of all those he owned that on going to hide from the press he'd taken the lot? But you'd think he must have one or more which was too big to carry around, one of the home-current-powered installations!

Well, that left only the bathroom and kitchen to check out, and after that, since Watson wasn't available, it might make sense to go back to the Carltons' commune and find out whether any of the other members of the group had taken the same road as Lilith and Leon Patrick.

The kitchen was just a kitchen. It held nothing in the least peculiar—

A man-shape moved across the open door.

A bright-red man-shape.

Dan froze, wondering frantically where he could hide, and had still not had time to decide on a course of action when the man-shape came back on its tracks. A pleasant, rather tired voice said, "Wally? Wally, is that you?"

And the new arrival glanced into the kitchen.

He was young—not more than twenty-five—and he was wearing a diving suit identical to the one in Watson's closet. In place of the lead-soled boots which should have gone with the suit, he was wearing ordinary rock-climbing boots with cleated soles. He had taken off the helmet and now clasped it under his arm like Ann Boleyn carrying her head around the Bloody Tower.

He smiled at Dan. "Oh, I thought you were Wally. Do you know where he is?"

"No, he's—" Recovering from the shock of being caught here, Dan's mind was suddenly working like a super-efficient computer. "He's keeping out of the way of the press. Someone went out at the club last night, and that was too public for the news to be kept quiet."

The stranger turned away, nodding, to lay his helmet on a nearby table. Warily, Dan emerged from the kitchen to join him in the lounge.

"Give me a hand with these bottles, will you?" the young

man said, unfastening the harness holding his oxygen supply. Dan helped him to wriggle free of the heavy tanks, and he stretched luxuriously.

"Not being able to crack the damned suit for twenty-four hours at a time is a bit wearing," he said lightly. "How big a splash has this affair caused, incidentally?"

"Enormous. It's on the way to being an international incident, and everyone and his uncle is out buying stardroppers."

Unzipping and peeling off his suit, the stranger sighed. "Well, I suppose it had to happen sooner or later. . . . By the way, I don't think we've met."

Superstitiously, Dan visualized crossed fingers and gave his name. The other nodded. "You're a member of the club?" he suggested.

"Only a recent recruit."

"Ah-hah. Well, I've been away up at Sixty-one so much lately it's not surprising I don't know you. I'm Robin Rainshaw, in case you hadn't guessed."

XVI

The rigid control Dan had imposed on his mind held good. The matter-of-fact announcement was a tremendous shock, but he did not betray it by the movement of a single muscle. He only paused for a few seconds before he felt he could trust his voice to remain steady while he spoke again.

Rainshaw didn't notice. He was clearly very much at home here. Having dropped his diving suit across a handy chair—under it, he wore the proper long-john-like coverall—he walked into the bathroom and turned on the tub. Waiting for it to fill, he moved to the kitchen and helped himself to a plateful of salad from a dish in the refrigerator, and at once began to attack it as though he were starving.

The first thing to become clear was why he had accepted Dan's presence so calmly. If he was a close friend of Watson—as seemed obvious—he would know about the alarms, and since it took a specialist with Agency training or a burglar of exceptional talent to evade a Protex system, he would take it for granted that Watson must have let him in or given him a key.

Or that Dan had come by the same route he himself had used. . . .

Either way, Dan must be party to the secret—the stunning secret that powers gained from the stardropper *had* been understood, controlled, and put to use.

Without meaning to stare, Dan gazed at him in wonderment. He was a rather ordinary-looking young man: fair-haired, fresh-faced, the sort of person one felt would smile easily and often. He did not look in the least like a man who could walk into a securely locked apartment without bothering to use the door.

120

But then—what *ought* such a man to look like?

Half the plate of food had disappeared when Dan said, weighing his words carefully. "I met your father recently, by the way."

Rainshaw nodded. "How is he?"

"To be frank, he looked worried and overtired. And I think he's losing weight."

"The strain must be awful for him now," Rainshaw said, frowning. "I wish he could make it too—but I doubt if he ever will, not unless we find some painless technique for overturning the preconceptions of a long lifetime. I even wish sometimes that I'd been hardhearted enough not to tell him I'd gone out, but I thought it would be even worse for him to think I was dead, or gone for good."

So Dr. Rainshaw was keeping up a pose! In that case, Dan realized, his acting must have been first-rate. If he'd given away a hint of the truth, Redvers would doubtless have pounced on it, but he'd appeared to accept that young Robin had merely disappeared.

Merely! It was shaking Dan to the roots of his mind to demote that, which only yesterday he'd regarded as incredible, to a commonplace by contrast with what he now knew was possible.

"Where did you say you'd been?" he ventured, and wondered whether he should add "this time." He decided against it, as Rainshaw showed no sign of finding the question oddly phrased.

"Hmm? Oh! Sixty-one again. Sixty-one Cygni."

This time the shock was worse yet. Fortunately Rainshaw was still preoccupied with eating and failed to remark the reaction Dan now could not conceal. Because 61 Cygni was a *star*, and not just any old star, either, but one which had become famous because there astronomers had ascertained the existence of an extrasolar planetary system. Oh, it hung together! The red diving suit, with its own air supply presumably because the alien atmosphere was unbreathable, not needing to meet the specifications of a suit for actual spaceflight because it wouldn't be exposed to vacuum or radiation and moreover was far cheaper and easier to obtain; the color slides of which Watson kept such a big collection, which showed scenes Dan hadn't recognized—small wonder, if they hadn't been shot on Earth . . .

And the man could come home (in a flash?) as calmly as from a walk around the block. *That* was the most shocking part of all.

But no one could adjust to such a vast change in his perspective on the universe without a chance to digest the implications undistracted. Here, illegally in a stranger's home, was no place to try and reason it all out. He would have to prompt, and probe, and discreetly ask innocent-seeming questions, for as long as he dared, and the task was made doubly difficult because he simply didn't know how someone in the position Rainshaw automatically ascribed to him ought to react.

"How was it, this trip?" That should be innocent enough, surely.

"Interesting, but not very exciting—Christ! I left the tub running!"

"I'll turn it off!" Dan said, and hastened to attend to that triviality. He was just in time; the water level had reached the overflow pipe. Returning, he added, "You were saying—?"

"Thanks. Yes, interesting, naturally, but . . ." Rainshaw shrugged, pushing away his empty plate. "The Earth-type planet of the system matches our gravity very closely, of course, or it wouldn't be such a convenient trip. But we're going to have to look a lot farther afield for our friends who originate the signals. I think they're most likely on planets belonging to far older stars than ours—Population II, perhaps. There may well be no one except ourselves in this entire area of the galaxy who's made the big breakthrough."

Inspiration followed the words in Dan's mind. Grasping at half-remembered scraps of information—from *Starnews*, from casual conversations—he suggested, "You mean we're sort of prematurely arrived on the scene?"

"Oh, I'm sure of it. If my old man hadn't chanced across the stardropper, it might have taken us another million years of evolution. Still, there's nothing to be ashamed of in taking a technical shortcut. That's always been our particular gift—gadgetry."

"So there's definitely nobody home at—uh—Sixty-one?"

"Not so far as we can determine. Of course, we haven't had the facilities to mount an exhaustive search, but on the face of things it's unlikely. The general level of evolution suggests Earth as it was half a million years ago, and it may not even be on the same course as ours took, because we're known to be allergic to one of the basic protein complexes of the local vegetation. I found that out the hard way, as you may have heard."

In mid-word he was overtaken by a burp, and looked dismayed, but interpolated an apology and an engaging grin. "Got a cigarette?" he added.

Dan fished in his pocket for his current pack. Seeing that it was an American brand, Rainshaw said as he bent his head to accept a light, "You are American, aren't you? Thought you must be. How are things your side?"

Dan covered the moment's hesitation he needed to frame a safe reply by lighting a cigarette for himself. He said finally, "Well, it's anyone's guess what the impact of today's news is likely to be. Panic, possibly. But until this thing happened it was very quiet compared to here. I got into this through being slightly acquainted with Berghaus" —no harm in dropping that particular name; it might improve his precarious standing with Rainshaw—"but I'm a real novice, I must admit, compared with you. It just so happened that . . . well, I was sitting right next to the man I told you about, who went out at the club in the full view of about fifty people."

Rainshaw sighed. "Yes, I wish we could have kept that from happening for at least a little while longer, but it was a calculated risk. . . . Was it a good one or a bad one? And was it anyone I know?"

A good one or a bad one? Dan failed to see the right answer for a second; then of course he realized. "A bad one, I'm afraid. Unmistakable. And it was a man called Leon Patrick!"

"The hell it was!" Rainshaw stared at him. "Poor bastard! I'd never have expected him to make it anyway—I mean, he's about my father's age, maybe older—but it's a dreadful shame he had to be a bad one. Are you certain? Oh, that's absurd: you must be, if you were sitting next to him. I don't imagine that was very comfortable, was it?"

"You're damned right it wasn't. I got pitched clear off my seat by the—what d'you call it? Implosion?"

"Hmm!" Rainshaw tipped the ash from his cigarette. "In that case there's *absolutely* no doubt! Poor devil." He shook his head. "How did the other people react?"

"To be honest"—Dan felt he had to tiptoe his way here —"I was rather shocked. This man Jock Neill from Scotland was giving a very interesting demonstration—"

He broke off. Rainshaw's expression had changed completely. It had hardened into a look of intense suspicion, and his voice was correspondingly brusque.

"Who are you?" he snapped. "And what are you doing here?"

Stunned, Dan tried to rehear what he had said and decide what might have given him away. He was still struggling to figure it out when Rainshaw made to rise, and in the act of rising disappeared.

Dan swung around on his chair. There he was, at the door, inspecting the locks and the alarm. He would notice no signs of tampering from this side, so that was halfway all right. But his mind might leap to the bedroom window overlooking the fire escape. . . .

Rainshaw was gone again, flick-flick. And yes, there he was visible through the bedroom door; he'd thought of the window and was examining it. And now he was back, confronting Dan from just beyond arm's reach, his eyes like chips of stone.

"Well?" he rasped.

"Well—what?" Dan countered. He had to play the innocent for all he was worth, and it wasn't easy. He was terrified, and not ashamed of the fact. How could anyone not be, suddenly faced with a man who could go *instantly* from one place to another and even, on his own admission, to the stars?

He saw a flicker of puzzlement break through Rainshaw's suspicion. Logic: a stranger and an outsider ought to have had hysterics at that demonstration of teleporting. Dan's acting was proof against that, at least.

Seizing his chance, Dan said, "What's wrong? I was going to say I was shocked to find that some of the people at the club were more concerned about going on with the demonstration than worrying about poor Leon Patrick!

That woman Mrs. Towler in particular almost went out of her skull with fury when Wally Watson called off the rest of the meeting."

"Why?"

"Well, I guess she"—*watch it!*—"thought she was getting somewhere for the first time, and didn't feel like letting such a petty thing as a death stand in her way."

And success. The suspicion was going out of Rainshaw's eyes. Dan instructed himself to exploit his opening as quickly as possible. He put on an injured expression.

"What made you fly off the handle like that? Did you think I was—well, a burglar or something? Hell, you saw for yourself that door is locked and what's more it's got alarms on it. And can you honestly imagine anyone walking up that outside escape in broad daylight?"

"I'm sorry," Rainshaw said reluctantly. He resumed his chair and again tapped his cigarette on the edge of his plate. "It was what you said about Jock Neill's demonstration that took me aback for a moment."

"How do you mean?" What was the actual phrase he'd used? "Calling it interesting, you mean?"

"Yes." Rainshaw's hostility had faded, but it was still latent in his voice. He kept on staring at Dan. "There can't have been any more to it that there ever is to a club demonstration. And least of all at Club Cosmica. The means don't matter, do they? Only the signals count."

Dan, his mind racing, took another gamble. He said, "Well, the Mrs. Towlers of this world aren't to know that, are they?"

His head was threatening to spin with the illusion that he was playing some childish game of forfeits, instead of fencing in a deadly serious duel of words. His quick improvisation seemed to have saved him so far. Rainshaw began to relax.

"Yes, I see what you mean," he conceded. "*She's* never going to go out—not even as a bad one. More likely she'll wind up in a mental home."

His tone was once again pleasantly conversational, though tinged with what seemed like genuine pity for Mrs. Towler and the likes of her. Dan felt a wave of relief wash through his mind.

Too soon. But there was nothing on—or off—Earth that he could do to help that.

For there was Watson standing behind Rainshaw's chair, more suddenly than a conjuring trick.

A long second ticked away, while Dan thought of the way Watson had dismissed Patrick's disappearance—denying that he was a callous man, and yet using such a harsh phrase as an epitaph for the vanished man that it had seemed brutal: "I simply have to face the fact that he wasn't *better*."

Well, now he was trapped. And you couldn't run away from a man who could interpose himself instantly between you and your way of escape.

But he desperately wanted to try.

As he—what would one call it?—materialized?—good enough—materialized, then, Watson had been in the act of stretching and yawning, as though fresh from an extremely tiring task. The moment he recognized Dan, however, he snapped to a posture of alert tension, and his eyes narrowed with menace.

"How the hell did *you* get in here, Cross?" he barked. "Robin, did you—?"

Rainshaw jumped to his feet, nearly upsetting his chair. "What? Wally, you mean he's not a friend of yours, not—not *one of us?* But I found him in here when I came back, and so I naturally assumed..."

"No, he's definitely not one of us," Watson declared. "He's an American, posing as a novice stardropper fan, who turned up in London a couple of days ago." (So short a time? It felt like an age.) "But I'm bloody certain he isn't what he's pretending to be. Well, Cross?"

Backing away, Robin Rainshaw looked almost comically crestfallen. He said, "I may have talked too freely, Wally. I thought he must be—"

"Can't be helped." Watson brushed the apology aside. He looked agitated, and his manner was brusque. Before he could speak again, the phone began to ring insistently; he shot a glance at it and Dan saw the hook switch move in twice, making and then breaking the connection.

Oh, God. He can move things at a distance, too....

"I warn you!" Watson said, his patience snapped by the interruption. "I want to know who you are—whether you're dangerous or just nosy. And I want to know this minute!"

Dan's mind was a total blank. He was trained to resist interrogation by any conventional torturer, but faced with —well, with *superman,* there was nothing he could draw on for assurance.

"Come on!" Watson barked. "You know some of what we can do! How would you like me to pick you up and hang you a hundred feet above Oxford Street until you talked? You'd have to be bloody quick, wouldn't you? You're heavy, and I'm already pretty tired, so I might have to let you drop without warning! Want me to show you? *Do* you?"

Rainshaw made as though to voice an objection. Watson silenced him with a glare.

"All right," he said to Dan after a pause. "You've had your chance. See how you like this!"

There was a kind of snatching sensation—not feeling that someone had taken hold of him, but more that all of his body was being moved against his will, like the express-elevator feeling but *sideways.* By reflex, Dan resisted, and for a moment he was seeing blackness.

Blackness?

Not just the lack of light caused by blinking, though it lasted no longer than a blink lasts, but blackness of an intensity he had never imagined: *dazzling* blackness. His eyes stung. His whole skin felt as though it had been pounded with wet leather straps. There was a straining tension in his ears, and he *had* to exhale as though he had been punched in the belly. His sinuses hurt like blazes, and he was simultaneously baking hot and freezing cold.

But he had seen something in the blackness, very sharply thrown into relief, like a fantastically overexposed photograph. He had seen a shape like a spreadeagle man.

And all this happened so quickly he had no time to be puzzled by it before there was light again, and he found he was not facing Watson and Rainshaw. He was in the same room with them, and they were just turning to each other with expressions of blank amazement.

"But he can!" Rainshaw said, and then, seeing where Dan was, swung to look at him and changed the words. "But you *can*!"

XVII

Into the frozen tableau the phone bell stabbed again, a dagger of brilliant sound. Watson stopped it this time without even looking toward the instrument.

He said, "I think—"

And broke off, putting his hands to his forehead.

Rainshaw, not less taken aback, said, "But I thought that was impossible! I mean, I'll swear that was a first time—it *smelled* like a first time! And no one has ever gone out for the first time when not actually listening to a 'dropper!"

Watson rocked back and forward on his heels. He said, "I think this man is an exception. An exception to everything. Cross, Cross, for pity's sake, *who the hell are you?*"

Dan wiped tears from his tortured eyes. He did not understand. He did not know how it was he had gone from where he had been, facing Watson, to here on the other side of the room; he did not know the meaning of the vision of darkness that had seemed to punctuate his journey. And all that mattered now was that Watson and Rainshaw apparently did know what this crazy pattern added up to.

He shivered, as though belatedly responding to a gust of ice-cold wind, and said in a voice that creaked like an unoiled door, "I'm an operative of the United Nations Special Agency."

"Thank goodness for that, at least," Rainshaw said, forcing a chuckle without humor. "I was half afraid you might be one of those bastards from the Blue Front who've been infiltrating the club recently." He glanced at Watson, but the older man disregarded him.

He said, "Are you really a stardropper fan, or are you using that Binton of yours merely as cover?"

"I was given a stardropper by my chief about four days ago. I never more than dabbled before then."

"Then all I can say is, you've set a record for speed of assimilation which is absolutely unbelievable." Watson was recovering his poise. "Robin, can you think of anything to explain it? Congenital predisposition? And you needn't have worried about the Blue Front, by the way: Ferrers and people like him will never make it, or if they do they'll have to give up their narrowminded prejudices. Xenophobia and this can't coexist."

Rainshaw bit his lip. Now the first panic reaction was past, Dan felt the two of them were regarding him as some sort of natural curiosity. He burst out, "Will you for God's sake tell me what this is all about?"

Watson hesitated. "First, you tell me something," he said. "What happened just now, when you went from here to there?"

Dan summed it up briefly.

"Fine!" Watson said with an air of satisfaction. "No one could have dreamed *that* up without seeing it. Fantastic that you should actually have spotted one of the failures, though!"

"Failures?"

Watson nodded. "Perhaps it was even Leon Patrick, poor devil—though come to think of it, it can't have been: the point must have shifted by now. So more likely it was someone we don't know about who went out near here a little while ago. They're making it thick and fast now. It looks as though all that was needed was one key event to tip a lot of people past the point of incredulity. Which of course was what we guessed might happen . . ." He looked suddenly tired and sad, and moved to take the chair Rainshaw had been using.

"Explain things to him, will you, Robin?" he added over his shoulder.

Rainshaw, not taking his eyes off Dan, licked his lips. He said, "Ah . . . well, just now, you 'went out.' That's to say, you found yourself at that particular point between here and the sun—in empty space—where the potential of the solar gravitational field is equivalent to that here in this room. Through luck, or subconscious understanding of what had happened, you were able to come back before much harm was done. But I see your eyes are watering, and you came back gasping like a stranded fish, and you'd be bloody well advised to go to a drug store right away and get a heavy dose of Radinox or some other reliable anti-radiation drug—"

"I have some in the bathroom cabinet," Watson muttered. He rose ponderously to his feet. "I'll fetch it. And a broad-spectrum antibotic, too."

"What for?" Dan demanded, still hopelessly muddled.

"You were out in space," Rainshaw repeated patiently. "Without a spacesuit, what's more! You were exposed to the full unshielded ouput of Old Sol, and that's fierce! Quite apart from any cellular damage, there's the risk of some of your tolerated bacteria having been mutated—though admittedly you're much better off than if you'd gone to the same place in a spaceship, because the primary cosmic just went through your body as though you were a window, and inside a ship you'd have stopped a lot of slow secondaries. . . . Hell, I'm rambling! Give me another cigarette, will you?"

Numbly, Dan complied, waiting for sense to emerge from what Rainshaw was telling him.

"All right," Rainshaw said, breathing his first smoke. "Now this is what happens to the bad ones, as we call them. A person 'goes out' to that equipotential point, just as you did, for the excellent reason that it's the easiest place to aim for in the entire solar system, far easier than an equipoint on the surface of the earth, for example. What's more, it has the attraction of being a spectacular first jump. There must be some sort of subconscious admiration for space travel built into the human psyche, I suppose. But what's most important is that accurate aiming over short distances takes practice. Out there, there's nothing to crash into and accuracy follows automatically from the least-resistance principle.

"But at that stage a bad one panics, or fails to comprehend what he's done. And he dies. There's no helping him. I wish there were!"

"Me too," Watson said gruffly, returning from the bathroom with a glass of water and two small capsules, one yellow, one pink. "Here," he added to Dan. "Swallow these."

Dan complied, and Watson continued, "Yes, I really do wish we could help the bad ones! Someone like Leon . . . he was a good friend of mine, and I liked him. But he simply didn't have the mental flexibility which you have, for example."

"But I still don't see—"

"What makes you a good case, and him a bad one?" Rainshaw supplied. "Nor do we, really. Except we know it has something to do with openmindedness. But what happens to a good case, like yours, is easy to describe, even if we can't explain it.

"Out there at the equipotential point, a good case recovers from the initial shock, recalls what he did to arrive there, and repeats the journey in the opposite direction, back to Earth."

"But—my God!" Dan wiped his forehead. "It takes energy to move a man from the surface of the earth into orbit!"

"Certainly it does," Rainshaw said. "But simple reflex balances the energy account. Think for a moment, and you'll see that the most economical way for someone who goes out quietly is to exchange places with an equivalent volume of air."

"You mean like from one point on Earth to another?" Dan was struggling, but little by little memories that seemed to be engraved in the bones and muscles of his body, rather than in his brain, were taking on a pattern.

"Primarily," Rainshaw agreed. "And that, more or less, is what you did, overelaborating slightly because you took a long way around . . . but then, so did I, the first time. And there was scarcely a whisper of sound during your trip. You're good—or you're going to be, once you've practiced enough."

"But I don't know *how* I did whatever I did!" protested Dan.

Watson broke in before Rainshaw could answer. He looked as though a great light had dawned on him. Pointing a finger at Dan, he said, "I think I know what made the learning process so rapid in your case. If there's one thing everyone knows about the Special Agency—from TV and movies—it's that each of the operatives has a personal-association code, tailored to the individual. Is this true?"

"Yes, though I don't see—"

"And it's hypnotically locked away from consciousness until it's triggered by some prearranged signal?"

"Yes! *But I don't see—*"

"Then that makes sense," Watson said, continuing as though Dan hadn't spoken. "Memory of a code like that, circulating nonstop in your subconscious, would free you from the worst tyranny of language and short-circuit what I suspect to be the biggest obstacle most people meet in trying to comprehend stardropper signals." He sat forward on his chair with an earnest expression. "Human knowledge is transmitted in words, yes? Arbitrary labels chosen by someone other than the user! Even neologisms are made up of spare parts, so to speak—they're not truly original. But a personal-association code refers directly to the user's private experiences. That's halfway to the basic prerequisite for understanding stardropper signals. You see, those signals aren't labels, like words in a human language. They're analogue processes, corresponding to real experience on a one-for-one basis. Right, Robin?"

Rainshaw nodded. "What you have to do," he amplified, "is learn how to—to *skew* them along a human axis. Some of those minds out there are a hell of a lot different from us, that's for sure. But they're still minds!"

Dan sat in silence for a moment, thinking of Lilith's pathetic attempts to make him understand why she was so determined to get back to stardropping.

Lucky kid! Going out quietly, presumably she must have survived! But it feels like a million-to-one chance!

"I knew a schoolkid who made it," he said after a pause. "Why could she go out where so many adults have to fail?"

"Fewer preconceptions is the simplest answer," Watson grunted. "But also one of the least accurate. It's partly that the experiences the signals correspond to are, in everyday human terms, impossible; and partly that one man plus one stardropper is like one fisherman trying to catch *only* one species of fish in an ocean that contains thousands, all hungry."

"The cocktail-party factor," Dan suggested.

"That's exactly what we call it," Watson said with some respect. Dan decided not to say how he knew that already.

"And if you lose track of your fish?" he said.

"You may make no sense of the signals at all; you may be permanently tantalized by a suggestion of meaning, a hint of sense, until you can't stand it any longer and break down. Or you may do something stupid like trying to stardrop under drugs, and you'll almost certainly become clinically insane. I say clinically: what I mean is that you may very well make a *terrific* breakthrough, clear into the psyche of some alien species. But what consolation is it to find yourself thinking like a green Sagittarian octopus when you *aren't* one?"

Rainshaw gave a bitter chuckle. He said, "Christ, I'm glad I'm not a psychiatrist right now!"

"Me too," Watson murmured.

"But if you succeed," Dan said, frowning, "what it means is . . . ?"

"That you've kept hold of one strong, clear sequence of signals long enough to acquire the vicarious experience needed to interpret alien techniques into human actions."

Dan remembered Angel's metaphor: "Tell me how it feels to ride a bicycle." She was probably going to make it if she had formed that close an analogy. He wondered in passing whether she knew what had become of Robin, as his father did, or whether she had given him up for lost.

"The clearest and strongest signals," Watson was continuing didactically, "presumably come from the most highly evolved minds. Now, as Jerry Bartlett was saying last night, evolution is a matter of improving one's species' degree of control over the environment. The commonest talent to learn from stardropping, to start with, is teleportation, and the next commonest is telekinesis. I have both of these, as you noticed, and I think I'm on to something else I don't have a name for—but that's by the way. The point is: control of environment is also control of probability. I can't put the mechanics of it into words for you, because it doesn't belong in words; if it did, you wouldn't have to learn it through a medium like the stardropper.

"But I can give you some hints. You know, for example, that there's a vanishingly small statistical likelihood that a given subnuclear particle might be elsewhere than where it's observed to be? This can only be demonstrated on a microcosmic scale—or *could* only be, until the advent of the stardropper."

"Jerry told me you'd said he was wasting his time on micro effects, when there were macro ones under his nose," Dan said.

"And there are!" Watson smiled. "Aren't there?"

"I have to believe it now," Dan sighed.

"I should bloody hope so. And I hope Jerry will catch on soon, too—we need people like him. I think he may, what's more. Last night he showed signs of appreciating that control of one's location by an act of will is the terminal point of a continuous sequence, which begins with toolmaking and the planting of seeds in spring against harvest time in autumn. It's a question of envisaging a future event, and taking the necessary present action to ensure that it's the desired outcome. It doesn't matter if we can't verbalize the action we're taking. We used fire for untold generations before it occurred to anyone to formulate a theory of combustion, and the early theories were wrong anyway."

"I'm still hung up," Dan said, his frown by now so deeply etched that his head was beginning to ache. "On this question of energy supply. I mean, to go from here to a *star*—it must take some fantastic expenditure of energy!"

"I let that slip," Rainshaw murmured apologetically to Watson.

Watson shrugged. "Fallacy," he said. "I'll show you why. It's another prime example of how traditional thinking can interfere with your accepting the information available from a stardropper. Not that it seems to have bothered you. . . .

"Imagine a planet as smooth as a billiard ball and totally airless—yes? Now imagine a satellite one millimeter above its perfectly level surface, in orbit. Is there any reason why it shouldn't continue forever without expending energy? I mean in ideal space; forget the other bodies in the universe."

"In orbit at one millimeter! But . . . yes, all right."

"At any given point on its orbit, it has the same potential energy as at any other, doesn't it?"

"Uh—presumably."

"I'm telling you. Moreover it has the same potential energy as any other satellite of the same mass orbiting any other perfectly smooth airless planet of the same mass. Okay? Now forget about its being in orbit. That's irrelevant. It could equally well be in contact with the planet's surface, being carried around by its diurnal rotation. What's its potential energy if it's instantaneously removed to a distant point, and then instantaneously replaced where it was before?"

"The catch is in the word 'instantaneous,'" Rainshaw put in.

"The Berghausian continuum is real," Dan said slowly.

"The Berghausian continuum is real," Watson repeated. "It does not require distance to be covered in elapsed time. So, when you yourself went out to the equipotential point between here and the sun, and returned, you expended the following energy: *one*, that consumed by your mental processes in making an act of will, and *two*, that consumed owing to the difference in mass between your body and the volume of air with which you exchanged places. So long as there's inertia you can't avoid that. But since you're accustomed to moving—what?—a hundred and seventy pounds, by the look of you—every time you take a step, you didn't give it a second thought!

"There are points on the surfaces of planets throughout the universe to which we can go—or shall be able to, after practice and experiment—as easily as stepping across a room. An animal doesn't know how it converts food into energy, but it can run regardless. We'll figure out the nature of the process later. Meantime, we can have a lot of fun just doing it!"

"Most of it follows from Berghaus's hypothesis," Rainshaw said diffidently. "Actual instantaneity—previous action—separation with distance . . ."

"I was getting that!" Dan said, thunderstruck. "During Neill's demonstration! I was fumbling after just this kind of thing, and I was furious when I was interrupted by Patrick's going out!"

"In that case," Rainshaw said dryly, "no wonder you described the demonstration as 'interesting'! I'm sorry."

"Since when," Watson said, nodding, "I suspect that the whole area of your subconscious memory which is full of this memorized association-code has been analyzing the logical consequences. You've been, as it were, 'sleeping on the idea.' Any creative thinker knows about that sort of thing." He hesitated. "Do you think you could go out now, intentionally?"

"I—I'm not sure." Dan was hunting in his mind for clues to how he'd achieved his personal miracle. "I think what made it possible was feeling you about to—to lift me up and hold me over the street. But I don't know! Christ, I don't *know!*"

He put his hands to his head. There was a kind of earthquakelike, grinding sensation going on in his brain, as all his lifelong assumptions went to the scrapheap. You could walk to the stars. There were alien intelligences. There really were supernatural—no: *natural* talents. And, this being true, the world was a different place. His reactions had to change to accommodate these new facts. A few minutes ago he had feared and hated these men. Now the only thing which seemed important was that they had entered this strange new cosmos ahead of him, and might help him to find his way around.

Fifty questions were burning his tongue. He picked one at random and lanced it at Watson.

"And you? I mean, I know you have the talent, because I saw you arrive. But in that case why are you a store manager? Why don't you—?"

Watson cut him short with a smile. "I already gave you the answer. You just didn't realize how true it was. Through Club Cosmica and its sixteen provincial branches I'm in touch with literally thousands of stardropper fans, from trained scientists down to teen-age kids. The store itself has an international reputation and an international trade. It's an entirely practical way of keeping track of what's going on."

"I see." Dan glanced at Rainshaw, recalling what he'd said to evoke such fierce suspicion. "And the demonstrations and so on that you organize at the club are just a way of bringing particularly informationful signals to the members' attention?"

"In a way," Watson said judiciously. "The prime purpose of them is not to study the signals, but the audiences. You see—"

The buzzer on the door sounded. He glanced at Rainshaw.

"See you later," he said. It was a command. Rainshaw nodded and vanished without even bothering to rise from his seat. Dan's stomach turned over. It would take a long time for him to adjust to such a casual attitude.

"I think," Watson said meditatively as he moved toward the door—conventionally, on his feet—"that our caller may be a policeman. In view of your work with the Special Agency, it may well be someone you know."

"Redvers?" Dan said.

"That's right." Hand poised to unlock the door, Watson gave a glance around the room, and with another twinge of shock Dan saw Rainshaw's red diving suit vanish. "I would have mentioned, only we've not had time, that I went out for a purpose this morning. Me and a few friends. I think we achieved what we intended. Just! We've had to be a bit cruder than we hoped, but I think we left a small margin of safety." He was talking to himself rather than Dan as he opened the door.

Standing back, he said, "Hello, Hugo. Come on in."

XVIII

Two points occurred to Dan as Redvers came in—apparently unrelated, but in their different ways significant. First: *He called him Hugo, and I didn't realize they knew each other personally.* Second: *Maybe it always happens like this, but one thinks of the world-shaking decisions being taken in palaces or generals' tents, not in the familiar setting of a town apartment.*

Redvers, on entering, hurled a fat portfolio from under his arm at the seat of a handy chair, and rounded on Watson, his eyes burning. He had barely spared Dan a glance.

"Well, Wally," he choked out, "I suppose you're pretty pleased with yourself!"

Closing the door, Watson shrugged. "Moderately," he conceded.

"I see you got *him* on your side, too!" Redvers barked, gesturing at Dan. "That must make you bloody overjoyed!"

"I didn't do anything to convert him," Watson said peaceably. "He made it of his own accord. He went out."

What was all this about "your side"? Blankly, Dan stared from one to the other of them.

Slumping into a vacant seat, Redvers wiped sweat from his face. He said, "Ah, shit, what does it matter anyway? We haven't got much longer, that's definite. Seventy-two hours at the outside."

Whereupon his self-control broke apart and real passion flooded into his voice. "Jesus *God!*" he almost screamed at Watson. "Don't you realize what you've done with this —this *lunacy?* Do *you* know what this bastard's been doing all morning?" he added, swinging to face Dan. "Do you realize he's wiped out everything your Agency's been working for ever since it was founded?"

"What do you mean?" Dan jolted forward on his chair.

"I'm telling you! He's been showing off—appearing and vanishing in plain sight of everyone he could reach! Fleet Street! Piccadilly! Lime Grove television center! Piccadilly in Manchester!"

"And Fifth Avenue, and Red Square, and the Boulevard Mao Tse-tung in Peking, and a good few other places," Watson said as calmly as though describing a world cruise. "But I wasn't the only one, of course. There were over fifty of us working together. I couldn't have done it by myself—not in the time available. If I tried to go from here directly to the street, I'd be just as smashed up as if I'd jumped out of the window; the other way, it's as exhausting as running upstairs at full pelt."

His face crumbling with incredulous dismay, Redvers said, "It's driven you out of your mind, Wally. You don't seem to care what harm your so-called fun might cause! I suppose, now you've got your godlike powers, you don't sympathize with us ordinary mortals any more—you can just amuse yourself by stirring us up, like a man kicking an ants' nest to watch them run about in panic! You, Cross!" He shifted his accusing gaze. "What do you think the result is going to be?"

Dan got slowly to his feet, so appalled he could barely speak. He said, "It *is* lunacy! Why . . . ! Well, this is calculated to drive people crazy with fear. It makes a mockery of international frontiers, of all security, secrecy, and even personal privacy. Did you say seventy-two hours? I wouldn't bet on our having more than twelve!"

"Tell me why," Watson invited.

"Isn't it obvious?" Dan stamped his foot. "What government is going to risk the other side getting hold of the secret of teleportation ahead of them? You could be deliberately stampeding the world into war!"

Watson took a cigarette from a box on a table near him, but didn't light it. Holding it thoughtfully between finger and thumb, he said, "That's the general idea, actually."

"You are insane," Dan said, his mouth going dry. "Don't you know that at this very moment there's nuclear potential equivalent to—?"

"A hundred and sixty tons of TNT for everyone on

earth, man, woman, and child," Watson said in a bored tone. "Yes, it was in the papers. And enough bacterial toxins to kill everyone about three times, and enough chemical weapons to do the job twice more on top of that. I do follow the news, you know."

"Cross, for God's sake!" Redvers was almost moaning. "Is there any way to stop what this maniac has started?"

There was a curious empty feeling in Dan's guts. He had to shake his head.

And yet Watson remained quite composed, toying with his unlit cigarette. He said, "So you didn't get what you thought you would out of your stardropper—is that the sum of it, Hugo?"

Redvers crushed the heels of his hands against his temples, as though hurting himself might make him believe this was actually happening.

"What's that?" Dan snapped.

"Out of my stardropper . . ." Redvers said in a choking voice. "Damned crazy nonsense—oh, I've been such a *fool*! You were all I ever got out of a stardropper, Cross."

"Me? I don't understand."

"*I* wasn't so clever I could be waiting for a Special Agency man the moment he came off his plane. I heard about you beforehand, through the stardropper I used to own. Remember Grey, who spouted all that nonsense at you? I modelized him on the way I damned nearly got to be. I had this one piece of comprehensible information, that a big cross man was going to come out of the west and bring us the answer to our problems. By that time I was on my way to a breakdown, so I had myself treated, but I remembered very clearly, so when I saw the name 'Cross' on the plane's passenger list I checked up, and found out who you were by conventional means. And I wish now I'd never bothered."

He beat his closed fist into his palm. "Yet it seemed so reasonable! Who was more likely to help us than the Special Agency? And you still might have done it, I suppose, only this crazy idiot beat you to it, and thanks to him the world's going to go smash and all of us along with it."

Dan thought of hardened missile sites pitting the planet like the sores of some disease, of the submarines on patrol each with enough power to wipe out half a country, of the spy satellites and the canisters of botulinus and the pressurized tanks of nerve gas . . .

Any of a thousand individuals, perhaps ten thousand, might be driven to the irrevocable decision by what Watson had just done, and the moment one of those key persons' self-control snapped, it would let loose a worldwide landslide of disaster.

And yet a tiny itch of doubt remained at the back of his mind. Thinking he might be clutching uselessly at a straw, he turned to Watson. Surely, while a maniac might be calm, he wouldn't be so sardonically amused? Though if Redvers had been right he might by this time regard himself as above the affairs of ordinary men.

He looked a pleading question, and waited.

Holding his cigarette before him with one elbow on the side of his chair, Watson said meditatively, "if you hadn't lost heart, Hugo, and had yourself proofed against stardropping, you might not be so abjectly miserable now. From what you told me, I too figured out that this man called Cross might contribute toward saving us. I admit I didn't see what help he could offer until a little while ago, when he did something spectacular and unprecedented, but now he's told me who he is I can see all sorts of exciting possibilities. . . . Cross, have you worked things out yet, or are you still where poor Hugo is, stuck in a morass of pointless despair?"

A spark of wordless hope flickered in Dan's mind, but he could not bring himself to speak.

"Look!" Watson said in a commanding tone, and held the cigarette out at arm's length.

It disappeared.

"There are a practical infinity of points in the universe," Watson said didactically, "where the gravitational potential corresponds to that of any given point on Earth. There is positively nothing easier than to distribute a small object's constituent particles randomly among a number of those points. Compared with sending the object to a specific destination it's literally *no* trouble."

"And a small object can be—uh—pretty crucial," Dan suggested.

"Exactly." Watson smiled. No, this wasn't a maniac. This

was a man with so much common sense you automatically didn't believe it. Dan smiled back. He couldn't help it.

"What the hell do you two have to grin about?" Redvers demanded hysterically.

"Didn't you see that cigarette vanish?" said Dan. "Go on, Watson—spell it out. I think I know what you've been up to, but I'll need to hear you tell me before I really believe it's true."

"Yes, it's like waking up from a nightmare, isn't it?" Watson replied. "Tell me this first, though. I've been assuming that if anybody knows where it all is, the Special Agency does. Am I right?"

"Sure. I can tell you myself, down to a mile or two, the map references for every hardened missile site, every major stockpile of bacterial and chemical weapons, and every sizable troop concentration—correct up to about eight days ago, which is when I last went for a refresher. And if necessary I can get you into the Agency's local office, where they keep a computer solely to record movement of military material."

"What's been giving us headaches is the submarines," Watson said.

"No sweat. They need orders from their home bases. I can tell you how to put out the transmitters over which they'd receive the command to fire, and make it look like a coincidence of part failures. We'll have to make it snappy, though. There are a hell of a lot of the bloody things."

"What the hell do you expect?" Watson said with sudden vehemence. "We've been in the killing business for more generations than we can count—plenty of time to make it *impossible* to save the world! Only somehow, praise be, I get the impression that our hearts have never really been in it."

"How many—uh—how many people are in this?" Dan inquired. He had almost said: "How many of us?"

"So far, around three hundred, with more coming in all the time. We've had a terribly high wastage rate, but thanks to the new insights you've given me, I think we can start training people as soon as things have settled down. Use hypnosis to build an individual perceptual code for each separate subject. But that's for later." Watson chuckled. "Know where our best recruits are coming from? Government projects, eastern, western, and neutral! It's the first thing you seem to learn from a stardropper, even before information you can act upon—this sense that in a universe full of who knows how many intelligent life forms this is one small pebble and it's too small to contain narrow local loyalties. And, by the way—"

"Yes?"

"I was at the Chinese nuclear testing ground at Lop Nor this morning along with someone I think you know. A kid of about sixteen, seventeen."

"Lilith Miles?"

"That's right. She said I should thank you for lending her your Binton 'dropper. She went out, safely, the second time she tried it."

"Well, I'll be damned," Dan said slowly, staring into nowhere. He gave a sudden snort of laughter. "Oh, hell! I wonder how they're going to react to having kids with superpowers taking away their deadly little toys!"

Already he was thinking in terms of "they" and we." And yet that wasn't correct. Not *already*, but *always*. Watson was right to say that mankind's hearts hadn't been in the extermination business. It had always been "they"— someone else somewhere else—who did such stupid, dangerous things.

Watson turned to Redvers. "Have you caught up with us yet?" he asked.

Face buried in his hands, Redvers moaned a negative.

"Oh, for—!" Watson caught him by the shoulder and shook him bodily. "Listen, you idiot! Didn't it occur to you that this would be the first useful purpose we found to apply our new talents to? We've been planning this for months! I'm already certain there isn't going to be a war— not a nuclear war, anyway. There can't be. *There aren't any weapons left.* Ever since the news of Patrick's disappearance made it certain there'd be a crisis, we've been working that trick I showed you with my cigarette. Only we've been working it on plutonium cores in H-bombs, and military bacteria, and the remote-firing switches of ICBM's, and we don't intend to stop until we've taken the bloody bullets out of every soldier's rifle and scattered them to the four corners of the universe! And now let's see what the armies do with nothing but their bare fists!"

He turned to Dan and beckoned.

"Come on! I'm afraid we've missed something—I mean we must have, because there's so much of it! So let's get to the Agency computer you mentioned, as fast as we can."

"But—" Dan began.

"Oh, Hugo will get over it in the end," Watson said pityingly. "All of us will. This isn't fatal, after all. But the other thing was! Ready? I'll give you a shove, but I don't think you'll need much help—you have all the right reflexes waiting to be used."

He was right, as Dan discovered a heartbeat later.

And eventually, of course, there would be the stars.

THE END